THE KARSTEN FIELD TRILOGY BOOK 1

I0547642

SET FREE

GEORGE MICHAEL
LOUGHMUELLER

MillerWords, LLC
PO Box 1622
Mount Dora, FL 32756

Second Edition

For discounts on bulk purchases, please contact
MillerWords Educational Sales at
Sales@MillerWords.com

Printed in the United States of America

2 4 6 8 10 9 7 5 3

Library of Congress Control Number: 2016918398

ISBN: 978-0-9982986-1-0

To My Grandpa

CHAPTER ONE

COMING HOME

Frustration

Finding a parking space at the local mall in December frustrated Allan Howarth to the point of yelling. He growled through his teeth against the rolled up, frosted windows as cars darted about like rats scurrying for crumbs. An overweight, curly redheaded woman wedged into a spot that Allan had been waiting on for the past five minutes. It had taken the previous elderly driver that long to discover which key opened the door. When the old timer backed out toward him, wider than necessary, the other woman slipped her mini-van in despite his monotonous turn signal.

That failed attempt left Allan to circle the lot another time. He let his wife, Tina, and the kids off at the curb. At least he still liked the three of them enough not to force them to walk through the cold, sleeting weather. He let his temper simmer back down and thought for a moment how much he did like his family. Twenty-two years of marriage flashed before his eyes with what he felt were too few memorable occasions. This Christmas topped everything when Tina decided an eighteen-year-old girl and a fourteen-year-old boy were old enough to pick out their own presents.

No wrapping.

No unwrapping.

At best, he might get a *thank you*.

Allan thought he found a parking space. Luckily the sleet had not totally frozen on the ground, otherwise he would have slammed into a BMW parked sideways, taking up two spots. Obviously, the driver did not want anyone else parking too close. This elicited another gold-star swear from Allan.

Eventually, he found himself in the mall, straining to hear his wife's voice on his Android phone. Somewhere between canned Christmas Carols over blaring speakers and crying children, Allan found a place to meet his family. In the time it took him to find a parking space, Tina and the kids only made it through two stores out of the eight on their list. Gamestop only held interest for his son, Brett, but Allan crowded in with Tina and Alice. The four of them shouldered against some of the most aggressive suffocating shoppers Allan had ever seen. The video game store practically gave away merchandise with outrageous sales luring even the most credit challenged. Everybody claimed to have no money these days, but everybody seemed to be spending it. At the moment, Allan could witness that only Fox News believed the country was on the brink of financial ruin.

A burly man that would have looked at home behind the wheel of big rig bumped Allan out of the way so his small son could grab a violent looking military game.

"Merry Christmas," muttered Allan.

"What'd you say?" asked the burly man. "You need to watch your mouth."

The convenient appearance of a mall security guard insured that conversation did not go any further.

Aggravation

Luke-warm hotdogs at the food court sent Allan directly to the bathroom when they got home. Alice and Brett retreated to their bedrooms, where they spent the majority of their waking hours while at home. Tina ritually entered the evening's receipts into Quickbooks on her laptop.

"Hmmm, under a thousand," she seemed to cheer.

From his porcelain seat, Allan wondered what was under a thousand. He called, "A thousand what?"

Tina answered, "Our Christmas."

"It better be," replied Allan. He flashed on his own childhood and his parents' imposed ten-dollar limit.

"The kids only spent around eight hundred and forty dollars," added Tina.

Leaving his pants on the bathroom floor, Allan burst into the narrow master bedroom. He dodged the corner post of the king size bed that Tina insisted on. The only good that ever came from that bed was that it allowed extra space between them.

"Are you out of your mind?" Allan struggled against the urge to yell.

Tina looked slightly ashamed. She said, "I wanted them to have a nice Christmas."

"Christmas is ten days from now. You gave them our house payment," said Allan. "I don't get paid again until after the first. Who's going to keep the electricity on? Your book club?"

"I'm sorry. I didn't think..." started Tina.

"That's the problem, Tina, you don't think. You don't think about anybody but yourself. Why do you think we've been going to counseling these past six months?"

Tina grabbed Allan's pillow and a blanket from the bed. She shoved them into his arms and said, "It takes two to ruin a marriage."

Allan knew this was the universal sign for sleeping on the couch. It had become a weekly occurrence for him as they worked through their *little issues*. The marriage counselor had been her idea, but she seemed less vested in it than he was. Most of the time, Allan wanted them to make it through this rough patch, but sometimes he wished it could be over. He barely saw the kids anymore, so he couldn't miss them more if he was forced to move out.

Before he left the room, Allan said, "You need to take that stuff back in the morning. Right now, I need that money more than I need their happiness."

Invitation

The morning brought an unpleasant chill. Allan awoke, half off the couch, freezing. He wondered if someone forgot to turn on the furnace. He fumbled for the remote control on the coffee table, in hopes of checking the Weather Channel. The flat screen did not respond.

"What happened to my internet?" Brett called from the sanctity of his bedroom.

"What happened to *my* internet?" Allan corrected, under his breath. He did not enjoy the alpha male clashes that had become all too frequent with Brett. Apparently, the battery must not have run down on Brett's laptop, otherwise, he might have realized that all of their electricity was out.

Tina could not get her laptop going to check her payment records. She insisted that she paid the bill. Allan did not know whether to believe her. He walked outside in his house slippers, pajama bottoms and a windbreaker to see if the electric company put a lock on their meter. Instead, he found a snow-weighted branch had torn their cable completely off the house.

"Sweet, no school," announced Brett. A cell phone call confirmed that it snowed enough overnight to keep the buses from running.

"How am I supposed to get ready for work?" whined Alice.

"What work?" asked Allen. He felt perpetually like an outsider in his own home.

"Oh," Tina stopped Alice from answering. "She's been participating in a cultural program."

Allan felt his face go red. He said, "Don't tell me she's doing that modeling." Then to Alice, "We talked about this. Please tell me you're not letting random men take pictures of you."

Tina interjected, "It's not like she's taking off her clothes."

"I've done a few bikini shoots," offered Alice.

"You what?" said Allan. He had no other words. The feelings that swarmed his heart almost knocked him over onto the kitchen table. He had definitely looked at his share of pictures on the internet, but that had always been someone else's daughter.

"I am eighteen," said Alice. "I have a right to be happy."

"Not while you're living in my house," said Allan.

Brett managed to find his way into the kitchen at that moment. He said, "From what I hear, it might not be your house for long."

A sharp knock at the door brought the assorted bickering to a hold. Allan walked barefoot across the tan Berber carpet, building up an unwelcome static charge as he went. The small shock on the handle greeted him as he greeted their visitor. Allan answered the door, dressed in the same way he had gone outside, less the windbreaker. The diligent representative for the US Postal Service looked taken aback for being greeted by a shirtless, unshaven man with flaring nostrils.

"Um, good morning. Sorry to interrupt, but I have a Signature Confirmation letter," said the uncertain mail carrier.

"I'll sign for it," said Allan, snatching the man's pen. "Who's it for?"

The postman said, "Allan Howarth. From Shepherd Tunstile."

Closing the door, Allan wondered why the name sounded familiar. He sorted through random thoughts, working his way back through a dull gray tapestry of work drudgery and family arguments, until he reached a time when he might actually have been happy. The name belonged to one of his high school teachers, his favorite one, in fact.

Allan sliced the envelope with a butter knife and pulled out the contents. He unfolded the plain white paper to reveal a hand-written letter from his high school drama teacher, a man he had literally not spoken to in almost thirty years.

Dear Allan,

It has been too long. By God's Will, there is

little time to make amends for that now.

I knew you to be a youth of such promise. I had always prayed you would take up the yoke of teaching. Unbeknownst to you, I did follow your growth for some time. When I last inquired, I saw you made a man of yourself.

Now, God has seen fit to call me home. In these waning days, my dreams have been troubled. In my prayers, I feel that life has put up many fences for you.

I have a home in the country that I would like to give to you. It is modest, but it should suit a modest family. By now, I expect your babies are grown and about to bloom with all of the potential you once held.

Please grant the wish of a dying friend. His inner voice tells me it will bring comfort to your troubled heart. I have included the name of my legal advisor in this envelope.

Always,
Shepherd Tunstile

Allan started to crumple the letter. So much regret already flooded his life. His old teacher wrote about God. Why would God dump more guilt on him now when things seemed to be at their worst? Then a small card fell out of the envelope. When it hit the carpet, Allan could see the words "Ask for Ben Abrim". He picked it up and read an address on the reverse side. As far as he could tell, it was in the middle of nowhere, not too far from his hometown, but also not far enough to be forgotten.

Investigation

After two nights in a row on the couch, Allan had no interest in going to work. It had become easier to call in sick than suffer through the pointless anecdotes of his much-despised boss. Allan disliked his job with the same passion that he disliked so many things in his life.

The letter and card made their bed on the kitchen counter. The white paper glared like an alarm when Allan passed by to get his coffee. He decided at that instant that he would go out and see this property. Maybe he could flip it and make some easy money? Maybe he could talk to his drama teacher one last time?

Allan did not call his wife, nor text her. He left his own note on the counter, something he had not done since before the days of mobile communication. He threw together an overnight bag and pointed his car down the freshly plowed street. He hoped they were as diligent about clearing the snow in the little town of Karsten Field.

To Allan's slight relief someone did clear the snow from the main street. He spent the night at a Super 8 by the highway and made his early morning foray north on Route 7. The pavement ended at a two-story house that looked to have been converted into a bed and breakfast. Allan thought, at first, that he got the wrong address. This town appeared to be nothing but gift shops from an episode of the Twilight Zone. He doubted his own kids had ever seen that show. On one side of the street, he had his choice of candles or canned goods. On the other, two shops featured an extensive collection of blankets. There was one other restaurant aside from the B & B at the end of the street. This one was closed for the winter, according to the sign in the window. Allan also had his choice of parking spaces. No tourists joined him this Saturday morning.

There looked to be a few busy people inside a couple of the shops, but otherwise, the street was empty.

Allan did not know where to start. Then a man came around the corner near the end of the street, almost at a jog, as if he was late for something. The man wore a heavy wool coat, as black as his denim pants. A yellow button-up shirt flashed out at Allan with each brisk step. He guessed the man to be bald, but only his round face peeked out under his wide-brimmed hat. He sported a full-thick beard in which the gray attempted to stamp out the last of his brown hair. No moustache though, Allan had seen this type before. As the man came closer, he altered his walk to come directly to Allan. A twinkle in his eye made him seem friendly enough. Allan did not know if he was in the mood for friendly.

"Good morgen, stranger," said the short man. The top of his hat pushed him over the five-foot mark. Allan always paid attention to height. He used it to his advantage in many business dealings.

"Oh, hi," said Allan. "I'm looking for a Ben Abrim."

"Then God has seen fit to put me in your path." The little man beamed. "I am Ben Abrim. Which makes you Mr. Howarth."

This surprised Allan a little. He typically did not like to be the one with the least information. He started to ask, "How did you..."

"Ah, Mr. Tunstile told me to expect you," said Ben Abrim.

Allan pulled his jacket collar up against the biting wind, which did not seem to bother Ben Abrim. Other than making his cheeks rosy, he did not seem to notice the cold.

"Can you take me to him?" asked Allan.

"I can take you to his house," answered the friendly man.

"That would be great," said Allan, reaching in the backseat of the car for his bag.

"But, he is not there. He has gone home," finished Ben Abrim.

"Home?" said Allan. He processed the words. "You mean he died? I only got his letter two days ago."

Ben Abrim looked ashamed. He said, "I was instructed to deliver your letter only once we had put our brother's body in the ground."

Allan wanted a chance to maybe put one thing right in his life. He hoped he could rush in on the old man's deathbed and say sorry for missing out. Sorry for disappointing you, Teach. I know you had big plans for me, but I couldn't let them get in the way of my own plans. He actually practiced that speech most of the drive up here.

It did not make sense to leave without going to see the house. Allan sighed.

"Do you want to take my car?" he asked the rosy-cheeked man.

"Oh no. No motor vehicles past here," said Ben Abrim. "Besides, it's only three miles. We can walk."

Three miles of winter air burned Allan's lungs. He had not done this much exercise in the past month. Finally, they came to a small cabin on a gently sloping hill. Allan guessed it to be around two thousand square feet based on the outside shape. It could be big enough for a family of four, depending on how many bedrooms it had. He would be sure to put that in the ad.

Ben Abrim mounted the front steps and stomped his boots on the well-worn wood. He turned out to look back from where they came. He inhaled deeply, closed his eyes and mumbled something not intended for Allan to hear.

Then he said, "Welcome to Karsten Field. Your barn is down to the right. Back up that way another six miles is Elder Tibold's residence. His is the largest; yours is second largest. Most everyone lives within a mile or so of Elder Tibold. We are only fourteen families, if you count my house as one. Mr. Tunstile kept his distance since partaking of the outside world. Now back behind, you have about ten acres that should be good and fertile this spring. Mr. Tunstile hasn't worked the land in some time; so you will have some good honest sweat."

The whole time Ben Abrim talked, Allan stared at the snow-covered ground. He looked up and down the leafless trees, spotting the occasional squirrel and a speckled owl. He almost felt like someone else was speaking to him. Someone whispered for him to let go, relax.

"You will be considered outsiders. I pray otherwise, but not all residents of Karsten Field will welcome you. However, Mr. Tunstile told me God has a plan for you," finished Ben Abrim.

Allan shook his head. For a moment, he felt like he had fallen asleep. He turned to the short man and said, "Don't worry. We aren't moving in. I'm going to get this on the market once the snow melts. That's what I do. Real Estate."

Ben Abrim froze. He looked almost like Allan slapped him. "Oh, my apologies. By Mr. Tunstile's words, I expected you to be moving in. As it is, God opens every closed door. Being that you deal in real estate property, you may answer a different prayer. It is not for me to say, but Elder Tibold may want to speak to you regarding a matter of property that could change the lives of everyone in Karsten Field."

"That's great," said Allan. "I'll leave you my card and he can call me at the office on Monday."

"We don't use telephones," Ben Abrim informed him.

Before Allan could make any other excuse to leave, he heard a soft voice say, "Stay with Me and I will set you free."

The words did not come from Ben Abrim and Allan had not seen another person since they left the main street. Something about it gave him goose bumps. He suddenly felt warm, when the cold air had been nagging at him all morning. He wanted to ask Ben Abrim if he heard it as well, but the man's face revealed that he did not.

Instead of asking about the voice, Allan said, "Screw it."

"Oh, this house is made with Amish craftsmanship. We don't need screws," Ben Abrim replied.

"I meant..." began Allan. He laughed, a solid body-shaking laugh. It occurred to him that he had not laughed like this in at least a year. He continued, "Never mind. I think you better let your Elder Tibold know we're going to be moving in."

"Praise God," said Ben Abrim.

Emancipation

The reactions came as Allan expected them.

"No way!" Short and to the point from Brett.

"You cannot control my life like this," demanded Alice.

A solid week of sleeping on the couch from Tina.

For the first time in a long time, all three of them agreed on the same thing at the same time.

On Christmas Morning, Allan sat on the couch, wrapped in a blanket. He did not go for his usual morning coffee. He did not get dressed for work. Before he fell asleep the night before, he made his Christmas Wish. He did something he had not done since he was a child. He prayed.

With the near collapse and implosion of his family, he prayed simply for them to feel what it might be like to be free. He wanted to be free of so many wrong things in his life. He wanted to be free of a miserable job in a market where no one was buying houses. He wanted to be free to love his wife without fighting about finances. He wanted to be free to love his children without the electronic shackles of a world that had lost its way.

Tina joined Allan on the couch. She put her head on his shoulder, sadly, an unfamiliar feeling. She did not look like she had slept at all. He dreaded that she had finally made her decision to leave him. He thought a divorce would be the worst possible Christmas gift.

She surprised him with the words, "Okay, we'll go."

Nothing could have made Allan happier. He wanted to leave that moment. He quit his job three days before, so he had nothing else to wait for, with one exception. The family spent an awkward, mostly silent day waiting for December 26th so they could rent a moving truck.

With the truck backed into the driveway, they loaded all of their possessions.

Allan put in his computer, his forty-two inch

LCD TV, Blu-Ray player, CD player, golf clubs and more.

Tina had her laptop computer, bedroom TV, sewing machine, eBook reader and more.

Alice piled on bags of makeup, high-heeled shoes, an iPad and more.

Brett needed his XBox 360, his Playstation 3, his laptop computer, his Nintendo DSi and more.

After a day's drive, Ben Abrim met the moving truck at what Allan now thought of as the Karsten Field Emporium. He understood now that the real town existed beyond this portal to what Ben Abrim called the "outside" world. The friendly little man had arranged a wide sled and a workhorse to carry their possessions up to their new house.

A stern looking man stood with Ben Abrim. At first glance, he seemed two full feet taller than Ben Abrim. When Allan stood next to him, he guessed him close to six foot four inches tall. The man did not smile when he shook Allan's hand. He nodded, silently, and his gray beard poked at his own vest. He pushed his coat back to let his hands dip into his pockets. His gaunt figure seemed imposing and Allan knew this could be none other than Tibold Fencil, the Elder of Karsten Field. Two strapping young men behind Elder Tibold began unloading the Howarth belongings. However, they only put certain items on the sled and made another pile on the sidewalk.

Ben Abrim must have anticipated Allan's question. He said, "Elder Tibold has instructed the youths to remove any unacceptable items."

Allan watched the pile on the sidewalk grow faster than the load on the sled. He watched them drop things on the pile without concern for their financial or intrinsic value. They dropped his computer, his forty-two inch LCD TV, his Blu-Ray player, his CD player, his golf clubs, Tina's laptop, her TV, the sewing machine, her eBook reader, Alice's iPad, her bags of makeup and the majority of her wardrobe. The only thing of Brett's that made it onto the sled was his underwear. Most of his clothes advertised disturbing rock band images and obscene slogans. Allan watched the things, his possessions that he wanted and needed, turn into irrelevant garbage on the sidewalk. The things that he thought gave his life value and meaning suddenly did not seem so important.

The fact that Brett neither started a riot, nor had a heart attack amazed Allan. Something had come over his family. What looked to be the worst Christmas of his life may become the greatest. He had a chance to save his marriage and save his family. Coming to Karsten Field had set him free.

Elder Tibold did not accompany them to their new home. The youths kindly unloaded the sleigh and Ben Abrim showed them into the house. Tina came to Allan with the first question.

"Allan, there are only two bedrooms," she said.

Alice ordered, "I am not sharing a room with my younger brother."

Ben Abrim interjected, "Certainly not. By our

Ordnung, the men shall be on one side of the house and the women will sleep in the other bedroom."

Allan looked at his wife. Her expression demanded an explanation, but he had none. They would all be learning a new way of life. To this point, his family came along willingly. He could not explain their sudden change and feared it would not last.

He bid goodnight to Ben Abrim at the door. The small man said, "Once you are settled, I will discuss with you taking over Mr. Tunstile's duties at the school house."

"Me, a teacher?" laughed Allan. "I'm a real estate agent. Maybe old Shepherd wanted me to be a teacher, but that was thirty years ago."

Ben Abrim smiled, "Some things are not for us to decide. Please, don't burn your candles too low on the first night. Sleep well and welcome home."

His new friend left and Allan closed the door behind him. He reached to lock it, but there was no lock.

CHAPTER TWO

THE HAT ON THE WATER

Resistance

"There is no way I'm wearing that," demanded Brett.

Allan looked at the two felt hats on their table. Ben Abrim had brought them over quite early, around seven in the morning. However, he looked like he had already been up for a few hours.

He had said, "It is a small gesture, the first of many steps on your new path."

Brett picked up his hat. It had to be his because of the smaller brim. Allan understood in Karsten Field, their hats had meaning. The width of the brim represented age, while the height of the dome showed their place. Allan's stood no taller than Brett's.

"I am not wearing that," Brett said again as he carelessly tossed the hat back on the table. He looked genuinely angry, more so than his usual teenage angst. "All you ever do is ask me to trust you and then you do something like this."

Tina came out of the girl's room at the sound of the raised voices. Alice must still be asleep, deduced Allan.

"What's going on?" she asked groggily.

"He's having an adjustment problem," started Allan.

"I'm having a liar problem," corrected Brett. "First, you trick us to come to the middle of nowhere. Then these people steal our stuff. I'm not going to dress like an idiot too."

"Take it easy, son," said Allan.

"You take it easy. You're a liar, dad. Coming to this place and pretending to be someone you're not makes you a bigger liar," Brett said through clenched teeth.

Brett stormed back into the bedroom and slammed the door. Allan started after him, but Tina grabbed his arm.

"Give him some time. This is only our first day and I think we all have had a shock," she said.

"But that's my bedroom too," Allan said to his wife. Then he called to the closed door, "That's my bedroom too, you know."

Tina gently held both of Allan's hands in hers. She had not been this intimate in a while. He liked the feeling of her soft skin. It reminded him of how they used to hold hands everywhere they went when they were dating.

She spoke softly, "I was too tired to talk about it last night, but things are not exactly like you said they would be. Brett does have a point.

Where did they put all of our things?"

"Is that all you're worried about? Things?" asked Allan.

"You can't change somebody's life overnight and expect them to be okay with it," said Tina. She let go of Allan's hands. Although they stood only a foot apart, he felt alone without that contact. She continued, "Me and the kids were expecting to move into a cabin. I didn't think you meant a real cabin."

"You don't know anything about the Amish, do you?" he asked.

"I know they don't use electricity, but that doesn't mean we don't have to," Tina answered.

"Actually, it does."

Tina moved to look out the front window. The harsh whiteness of the snow silhouetted her form. Despite having two children, she managed to keep an attractive shape. Even if Allan lacked an emotional attraction to her, he still had a physical desire.

Allan explained, "I know this is the right thing. For me. For all of us. I literally thought about killing myself. Here, I see a chance to start over, to be free. We have to cut loose from everything bad in our old life. No more internet. No TV. I can't be like that anymore. Starting today, I am going to put all of my energy into you and the kids."

"That's going to take a lot of work," Tina said. She turned back toward Allan and smiled faintly. He knew she still loved him. He still loved her. Somehow, they had both buried those feelings.

Allan wanted to go over and hold his wife, but he hesitated.

Alice interrupted his urge. She said, "So, where's all our stuff?"

Allan did not know how much of their conversation she heard, but he did not think much. His daughter did not look awake as she entered the room barefoot. At least, Allan thought, the cabin stayed warm with the large wood-burning stove. The house had to be well insulated.

"Ben Abrim came by this morning," started Allan.

"Already?" asked Tina. "What time does the man get up? Five?"

"Yes," Allan said. "He shared some information with me about their Ordnung."

"Or-what?" from Alice.

"It's kind of like their rules. Things we have to do if we want to be part of them," said Allan.

"Like a rulebook?" Alice deduced.

"Yes, but it's not written down. We have to learn the acceptable behaviors. Ben Abrim said Elder Tibold is shunning us until we do."

"Wait," said Tina. "You want to become Amish? Isn't it enough to get away from everything?"

Allan spoke a little louder. He hoped Brett could hear his next words. "God has not been a big factor in my life. I think the only way I can love myself again is through Him. I know next to nothing about being Amish, but I am willing to learn. I think I need a connection to God so that I can have my connection with you all."

"How does that help me with my iPad?" whined Alice.

Allan tried not to lose patience with his daughter. He said, "It's in storage alright. Everything. All of our stuff is in storage. Elder Tibold does not think we will make it here. He had our things put in storage, so we can take them when we leave. I have the key, but no one is going near that stuff."

Alice let her head drop and rolled her eyes up at her father. She looked like she had more to say, but walked back to her bedroom. Before she closed the door, she said, "Wake me up when this nightmare is over."

Allan sat down at the table and Tina took the seat closest to him.

She said, "I don't understand you. I want to. I want to love you, but you do kind of scare me right now. Can't you find God in a church back in Des Moines?"

"I don't think that's where God wants me," said Allan. "I feel something here. I feel a purpose. That's something I haven't felt for years. This isn't a vacation for me."

Tina reached for him again. Twice in one day, Allan noticed. She held one of his hands in both of hers and rested them on the plain wooden table. She said, "You have two confused, upset children right now. You have always taken care of this family, so I am trying to trust you. You can't expect them to magically accept all of this." She put a hand on Brett's new hat. "Give them some time. Find out what you're supposed to do first."

Allan knew what he was *supposed* to do first. Ben Abrim had explained quite a bit earlier that morning.

Assurance

The small man's knocking awoke Allan much earlier than he would have liked after a day of moving. He left Brett asleep in his bed and quietly walked out of the room. Ben Abrim stood on the front porch with two hats in his hands and his own on his head. A large basket hung from the crook of his arm. He smiled as broadly as he did the first day they met. Allan wanted to know what could make him so happy all of the time, so he asked.

"That is a gift from God," said Ben Abrim. "I know where my salvation lies and, as such, nothing in this world can affect that. I lost my way for a time, much like you. My wife and I were never blessed with children and then I lost her not so long ago. I thought I could walk a different path, but it wound me around and back here. Mr. Tunstile was the only one, at first, to welcome me home. That is why I am always grateful to him and want so much to see you do good."

"Were you always his lawyer?" Allan asked.

"I've never been a lawyer. I've read a few law books, but nothing more," said Ben Abrim with a chuckle.

Allan thought back to Shepherd's letter, which referred to Ben Abrim as his legal advisor. "But Shepherd said..."

Ben Abrim turned his bright, innocent smile on Allan. He said, "Mr. Tunstile saw things in people that they usually could not. He may have travelled far from Karsten Field in his time, but rarely have any from Karsten Field been closer to God, I dare say."

Allan studied the man for a moment longer. He wondered why Shepherd Tunstile saw him to be a teacher.

"May I?" asked Ben Abrim, gesturing toward the open door.

"Oh, of course," said Allan. He had not realized they were standing in the cold morning air. Something in that air brought him such peace that he thought he could possibly spend the whole day outside. With almost a foot of snow, he thought better of it.

Ben Abrim placed his large, hand-woven basket on the table and unpacked a few items. He said, "I've brought you food for breakfast and dinner. We will have to make arrangements for more later. There are many things that need looking after today."

Inside the basket, Allan sorted through fresh brown eggs, a glass bottle of milk and various other jars. Then he inspected the hats.

"Please, wear these any time you leave your home," said Ben Abrim. "Elder Tibold is not so easily accepting, but some of our families will look on you favorably if you show them an effort. Amos Menlach and his wife, Sarah, are most interested in helping you get started. Sarah made you this gooseberry pie. And those two boys that helped move your belongings are their oldest of six. Mr. Tunstile taught all of the Menlach children."

Allan tried the hat and found it to be a near perfect fit. He placed it on the table next to the one intended for Brett. He said, "That's right. You want me to be the teacher. You know I have almost no qualifications for that?"

"Mr. Tunstile believed you had more than enough qualifications," corrected Ben Abrim. The look of seriousness on his face almost convinced Allan that he could be a teacher. "Besides, we have a bountiful blessing in having not one teacher, but two. Miss Mary Reece is young, but she is dedicated. She lost her husband in a farming accident before they had any children, so she has taken strongly to her students."

Knowing that Shepherd Tunstile helped Ben Abrim through a difficult time helped Allan see things a little more clearly. Obviously, Shepherd played a significant role in Ben Abrim's life and now that he lost his friend, Ben Abrim must have felt obligated. That would explain why he was pushing so hard. However, a tiny voice inside Allan told him it was not obligation or guilt. He was supposed to be here. Allan did not like the idea of teaching. He had not been around young kids in a long time. He would not even know where to begin.

Acceptance

"You didn't tell me he brought food," said Tina. She immediately left the table and went to the back half of the cabin that served as their kitchen. She began sorting through the box that Allan had moved to the counter.

Tina made a full breakfast like she used to do every Sunday when the kids were young. The smell of sizzling bacon brought Alice and Brett from their rooms. Neither seemed reconciled to their condition, but apparently, their hunger outweighed their anger.

Allan moved the black hats from the table without a word. He did not want a repeat of earlier. When Tina brought food to the table, they all sat together as a family for the first time in countless meals. Allan could feel a change in all of them, but he knew they were only at the beginning.

Between bites of scrambled eggs, Tina said, "I think you should do it."

"Do what?" asked Brett.

"Mr. Ben Abrim says your father is expected to be the new teacher, in place of his old teacher," said Tina.

"I don't know. I don't have any training. I would be so uncomfortable," excused Allan.

"Huh," said Alice. "In that case, I think you should do it too. If we're uncomfortable, then it's only fair that you are too."

He barely recognized his daughter with unkempt hair and no make-up. Alice looked like something out of an old family photo album. She reminded Allan of when she was six. He knew then she would grow up to be a beautiful woman. He gave her the tools and the attitude to control her life. These days, she used that against him whenever she could. Her wit and biting sarcasm told him that, even at eighteen, she was well equipped to take care of herself. She also had his pessimism. Alice wanted him to suffer as much as she was.

"Yeah dad," added Brett, "those kids would own you."

Some part of Allan hoped that he would have his family's support. He knew they were angry. He needed to prove that he made the right decision for all of them.

Tina smiled at Brett's comment. Then she added her own comment, but Allan doubted the sincerity of it. She said, "I remember when you did those seminars for new brokers. When was that, about ten years ago? I told you then that you were a great teacher."

Allen remembered it, too. He remembered being nervous and feeling unprepared. He tried to please an ungrateful boss by trying to show a room full of couch potatoes and shut-ins how they could work from home. He did not volunteer for that experience a second time. Allan knew teaching math and reading to a group of children would be different, but it still scared him. He did not know if he wanted that responsibility, especially if some of the parents did not want him there in the first place.

"Ha, a great teacher," snipped Brett.

Part of a male's instincts, somewhere in his genetic make-up, there is that uncontrollable urge to be the leader. The alpha male. As a father to a teenage boy, Allan had the unpleasant job of defending his position. For that reason, he stood from the table, dropping his fork on the empty breakfast plate.

"I'm going to do it," announced Allan.

None of his family members argued with him and in less than twenty minutes, he dressed and headed out the door, with his new hat on his head.

Allan had not seen the rest of Karsten Field yet, but he walked in the direction Ben Abrim pointed when he talked about it. Allan intended to go directly to Elder Tibold and tell him that he would be teaching. As he tromped along, he felt snow creeping into unfamiliar boots, melting with the heat and soaking his socks.

That did not slow Allan. He knew it was only about three miles and he had the whole day ahead of him. At first, determination drove him on, but after a mile, he found himself walking much slower. Allan noticed a total lack of sound around him. No traffic. No ringing cell phones. No people talking. The knee-deep snowdrifts dampened every noise. Allan looked at the thin trees around him and saw no sign of wildlife. He felt like he was walking on a road in a forest, but the swath between the trees was twice as wide as a normal street. He did not feel claustrophobic, but he did feel very isolated.

All at once, Allan existed in a world by himself. Some might be afraid of this, but Allan was not. He thought for a moment of a way to describe his new feeling. The best word he could think of was *exalted*. Then that small voice came back to him. He thought maybe it came from inside his head, maybe his subconscious, but that did not seem right. Maybe, he guessed, it came from somewhere deeper inside, like his heart. At the same time, it seemed to surround him and echo through the White Cedar trees scattered with Douglas Firs.

The voice said, "Set free."

Nothing else.

Allan heard no other words, no other sound. He did not know if it meant he had been set free or was he moving toward being free? The cracking sound of a branch caused him to spin around. Less than five feet away, he looked into the eyes of a white-tailed deer. Magnificent antlers stood out on its head like a crown. Allan could see the steam of breath bursting from its nostrils. He realized the deer expected to run into him as much as he expected to run into it. Allan's first instinct was to pet the deer. He reached out slowly. Surprisingly, the deer lowered its head as if it wanted to be touched. Within inches of touching the creature, Allan stopped. He wondered whether he should. Then a distant noise made the decision for him. It could have been a slamming door or even a gunshot. Either way, the deer snapped its head up, swinging the eight-pointed antlers around to scan for possible danger. Then the creature bolted into the woods and out of sight.

The experience gave Allan a burst of energy and he finished the journey faster than he expected.

The houses of Karsten Field surprised Allan. None of them looked like his cabin. They all looked fairly modern, white-washed with smoking chimneys. Allan saw no one outside, but he could sense activity in a few of the houses. In all, he counted eight houses, basically arranged in two rows, which left a type of road down the middle. The houses were situated further apart than in his old neighborhood, but they were all much closer than his cabin. Only one had a second floor, which told Allan whose house it was. He remembered Ben Abrim saying that Elder Tibold lived in the largest house in Karsten Field.

Allan made his way up to the front porch, but stopped a moment before he knocked. He could hear voices on the other side of the door. He instantly felt guilty for eavesdropping. His curiosity overshadowed his guilt, though.

"You are too easily swayed by the lure of the outside world, Ben Abrim," said Elder Tibold. The gruff, authoritative voice was unmistakable.

"This is not about me, Tibold, and you know it," shot back Ben Abrim. Allan recognized his voice, but detected less than the usual cheerfulness.

Elder Tibold continued, "You should not have given him the key. I, for one, do not expect them to last. However, you have made it easier for them to be tempted. Shepherd Tunstile took his rumspringa and, as far as I'm concerned, never came back. We cannot have these Englishers running all over

Karsten Field."

"Mr. Tunstile gave them his house. It is not for us to say otherwise. If he believed they belong here, then that is good enough for me," said Ben Abrim.

"And you would have an outsider teaching our children?" asked Elder Tibold.

"I don't know if he is a teacher, but I will trust the Will of God," said Ben Abrim. "I have seen this man's face. I believe he will answer to a higher calling when the time comes."

The unconditional support from Ben Abrim gave Allan some renewed confidence. He rapped sharply on the door before Elder Tibold could speak again. The rigid old man opened the door. He said, "What do you need, outsider?"

"I wanted to let you know that I will be teaching your children," said Allan. With no other words, he stepped down from the porch. He could see Ben Abrim beaming over Elder Tibold's shoulder.

"You will not last long enough to have an impact," called Elder Tibold. The raised voice brought a few others onto the porches of the other houses.

"I am going to do my best," said Allan. He flicked the brim of his hat in a farewell gesture.

Elder Tibold followed to the edge of his steps and spoke loudly to Allan, now in the middle of the road. The old man said, "You are not one of us. I doubt you are even baptized."

Allan felt a rush of energy through his body. It was not a flash of anger, like fighting over a parking space. It was the feeling of surety and confidence. He said, "Let's fix that right now. What do I do?"

Elder Tibold scowled. Ben Abrim stepped around the taller man and pointed down the hill. The short man said, "We do our baptisms in the river."

."Let's go then," shouted Allan. He looked at the other bystanders and they seemed equally as curious.

"This is not our way. He does not know the Dordrecht," stated Elder Tibold. "I will have no part of this."

"Then I will do it," said Ben Abrim as he bounded down the steps.

Most of the residents followed Allan and Ben Abrim to the river. The snow covered banks and floating chunks of ice did not slow Allan or falter his determination. The sense of peace and energy he felt with the deer returned. Allan did not even slow as he entered the freezing water. Ben Abrim stopped for a moment at the edge, but then followed Allan into the river. Ben Abrim stopped Allan when they were waist deep.

Through chattering teeth, Allan asked, "Now what?"

Ben Abrim must have decided on the short version. He grabbed Allan by the shoulders and said, "With ears that hear and a heart of understanding, do you bring forth genuine repentance and forsake all sin?"

Allan answered on instinct, "I do."

"Do you confess with your mouth and believe with your heart in one eternal, almighty, and incomprehensible God, the Father, Son, and Holy Ghost?" asked Ben Abrim.

"I do."

Ben Abrim finished, "And be you not conformed to this world, but be you transformed by the renewing of your mind that you may prove what is that good, and acceptable, and perfect, will of God."

The smaller man pushed the larger man into the water. With Allan submerged, Ben Abrim said, "I baptize you in the most worthy name of the Father, and the Son, and the Holy Ghost."

Ben Abrim helped Allan from the water. Allen saw looks of curiosity and awe on the faces of Karsten Field. One little girl hugged him. At the top of the hill, Elder Tibold watched silently.

Allan felt the cold air on his head and instinctively reached up. He did not feel his hat. Behind him in the river, he watched the hat on the water, floating away with the current.

Repentance

Shortly before sunset, Ben Abrim and the two Menlach boys brought Allan home safe on the same sled that delivered their acceptable possessions the day before. The older man wrapped Allan in two dry blankets.

In the growing darkness, Tina looked shocked as the men carried her husband into the cabin. To Allan's shuddering dismay, Brett laughed as a first response.

"Did you fall in a river?" he mocked.

Allan could not bring himself to respond. His whole body seized from the cold.

"This is no laughing matter, young man," Ben Abrim said with surprising sternness. "Your father requested the right of baptism and I assisted him. It was foolish to do at this time of year, but when God moves a man's heart, then His Will be done."

Brett stopped laughing immediately. He could only look at his father. Through bleary eyes, Allan detected it to be concern. Tina gathered more blankets and dry clothes while Alice made hot tea. The group ushered Allan into his bed.

Left behind in the front room, Brett had nothing more to say. He looked down at the hat that they expected him to wear. He picked it up by the brim with two hands. He flipped it over twice, then put it on his head.

He said, "Huh, it fits."

CHAPTER THREE

THE BARN INCIDENT

Burning

The smell of burned eggs filled the cabin. Tina's mother always told her it was impossible to ruin breakfast, but Tina somehow managed that on a semi-regular basis. Her mother said breakfast was the simplest meal of the day. "You only have to put it in the skillet and wait for it to get warm," she used to say.

Tina waited for the eggs to "get warm", but sometimes, she waited too long. Since moving to Karsten Field, her primary duty had become cooking. She did not have a fast food crutch to lean on, so she struggled to remember any tips and tricks from her mother and grandmother. When her children were still in elementary school, Tina never burned their Sunday breakfast. Over the last two weeks, she burned the eggs at least five times. That did not include any bacon, or the disastrous day she tried to make pancakes.

"This is not my fault," she told herself. She believed there could be no easy transition from an electric Whirlpool Gold to a cast-iron, wood-burning stove made before she was born. Not that she ever used the Whirlpool much, but that served as a good excuse.

In addition to burning breakfast, she now had a varied collection of burns and bruises on her hands and forearms. It seemed that every part of the stove got hot. One wrong move caused her to jump or yelp with that sudden flash of pain. The cookware left behind by Shepherd Tunstile had to be some of the heaviest pots and pans ever made. Tina could barely lift the Dutch Oven that she used to warm the soup for Allan.

Tina currently had two things for which she was thankful. One, she probably would have starved if not for Sarah Menlach. Sarah encouraged a few of the other Karsten families to share their winter stores with the newcomers. Sarah taught Tina how to manage the fire and keep it burning all day. She showed her how to store the food and measure portions. Tina always ended up with too much on the table because Sarah was used to cooking for her husband and six children.

The second thing that made Tina thankful was that Allan did not eat any of her food. Since his baptism, he had only eaten soup. She certainly was not glad that he fell ill, but only that he could not comment on her burned-to-saved ratio.

Thanks to Amos and Sarah Menlach, aside from cooking, Tina only had to tend to Allan. The

Menlach's made certain they had food and loaned their second eldest, Samuel, to oversee any chores. Their oldest, David, stayed to take care of the Menlach chores with his father. Brett and Alice reluctantly went to the Menlach house. Sarah assured Tina that her children would soon learn what was expected of them.

Having no idle children under foot left Tina to concentrate on her husband. She knew Allan long enough to know that when he got an idea in his head, his mind could not be changed. Even if she had been with him, she doubted she could have stopped him from plunging into that near-frozen river. As a result, he had been sick in bed for the past two weeks. Tina suspected he had pneumonia, but even in a weakened state, he refused to go to the hospital.

Healing

The time since Allan's baptism passed in a dream-like blur. He had no sense of the days, only a recollection of dark and light. Strange ideas danced in his head as he teetered on the edge of a severe illness.

When he decided to go into the river, he did not think of what might happen after that. He felt that he needed to prove his devotion. So instead of waiting for spring, he splashed into a near frozen river and lost his hat.

As he started to heal, things became clear. He remembered Ben Abrim visiting several times and the kind man even brought a replacement hat. He also left a few things for Allan to read. His wife's constant attention and warm soup became less abstract as his head cleared. Allan remembered that Tina wanted to take him to the closest Emergency Room, but he did his best to resist. Only in recuperation did Allan understand how truly sick he had become. His old self would have gone to the doctor on the first day.

In between fevered bouts of clarity, Allan read the Bible and the Dordrecht Confession of Faith. The words burrowed into his subconscious in this semi-lucid state.

"Without faith, it is impossible to please God."

It had been a long time since Allan felt that he could please anybody, including himself, but especially his wife.

"He called them again to Him, comforted them, and showed them that with Him there was yet a means for their reconciliation."

Allan believed he had been called. He heard that voice the first day he came to Karsten Field. He felt that energy on the bank of the river. As he lay in bed, shivering at one moment and sweating the next, he felt a connection to something he could not explain. Allan wanted to hear that voice again and he wanted to know to whom it belonged.

With Tina as his constant caregiver, Allan's thoughts turned to her. He wondered what she thought of his baptism. He never expected her to be his nurse. He thought they were past that point in their marriage. He actually expected it to be an opportunity for her to take the kids back to Des Moines. Maybe, he hoped, they still had a chance to work through their problems and stay together.

"So the believers have likewise no other liberty than to marry among the chosen generation and spiritual kindred of Christ, namely, such, and no others, who have previously become united with the church as one heart and soul, and have received one baptism."

This bothered Allan.

In the first place, they were married at the courthouse. Would the people of Karsten Field see that as a true marriage? Allan suspected Elder Tibold would not. It bothered him more, though, that Tina showed no signs of wanting to become Amish. He remembered one of their last coherent conversations. Tina stated that even if they lived like the Amish, that did not mean they had to become Amish. She wanted him to find a church back in the city. Allan believed that would not fix the hole inside his heart.

The last thing Allan read made him think of the strict and moral pointed face of Elder Tibold. Ben Abrim said that Tibold was shunning them and did not believe they could make the transition to the Karsten way of life.

"Therefore, we must not count them as enemies, but admonish them as brethren, that thereby they may be brought to a knowledge of and to repentance and sorrow for their sins, so that they may become reconciled to God, and consequently be received again into the church, and that love may continue with them, according as is proper."

Allan read this two ways. First, Elder Tibold only wanted to protect his church and hold back any temptation from the outside world. Second, Allan needed to change his own thinking. He saw Tibold as opposition, someone to prove himself to. He began to understand that the only one he needed to prove himself to was God. He hoped Elder Tibold would accept him once he was reconciled.

"For, if he is needy, hungry, thirsty, naked, sick, or in any other distress, we are in duty bound, necessity requiring it, according to love and the doctrine of Christ and His apostles, to render him aid and assistance; otherwise, shunning would in this case tend more to destruction than to reformation."

Allan knew that Elder Tibold would not wish him harm, but he may see a more direct path in having them gone. Allan could not wait to get his strength back. He planned to ask Tibold for guidance. If the old man would not help, he knew Ben Abrim would. Already, several other families had been sharing their food and other necessities.

Along with the books, Ben Abrim included some notes on the Karsten families. Allan read the names of the families with school-age children: two Fencils, Menlach, Miller, two Ottos, Gundy, Kurtz and Troyer. From nine of the fourteen families, twenty children currently attended the Karsten Field School. That did not seem like an unmanageable number. Besides, he expected there would not be the same type of disciplinary issues like he saw when his kids went to middle school.

After a short bout of delirium and two weeks rest, Allan finally felt strong enough to get out of bed. He knew Tina would be preparing his afternoon soup, so he wanted to surprise her. He came out into the main room as she poured the hot liquid.

"Hello nurse," he said jokingly.

This must have startled Tina because she dropped the bowl. Cabbage soup splashed across the wooden floor.

"What are you doing out of bed?" she demanded.

"I feel great. Really," Allan said. He offered a hug as an apology.

Tina stooped before Allan could reach her. She sopped up the soup as best as possible with a tattered blue dishtowel. She tossed the now empty bowl into the sink basin and jerked at the old pump handle. A trickle of water greeted her waiting towel. Allan reached over her and steadily pumped the lever two more times. An even flow of cold water streamed out into the sink.

"It's not that easy for the rest of us," said Tina. She turned away from him and sat at the table.

"What does that mean?" asked Allan.

"Everything has been so easy for you. Leaving everything behind, coming up here. I'm used to running water. The Menlachs have indoor plumbing," she lamented.

Allan tried to joke again, "Always trying to keep up with the Menlachs." He thought it was a clever substitution on the old phrase, but he did not get even the hint of a smile from his wife. He added, "At least we don't have to go outside to use the bathroom."

"You don't get it, do you?" asked Tina.

He could see the look on her face, read the emotion in her eyes. After this many years, Allan still could not interpret the silent, secret language of the most dangerous of predators known as woman. He did not know what she meant, so he said what any well-trained husband would say, "Of course I do. I only want you to be happy."

"Do you Allan? Or do you want me to be quiet and smile, so you can be happy?"

This stung, deeply. Allan honestly wanted his wife to be happy. He saw their move as a chance to reinstill something they once had. They must have been happy once, he wondered. He faltered for a moment with the thought that they maybe never really shared anything. He did not want to believe that.

"But..." he started.

"There are no buts," Tina interjected. "I can tell that you don't understand. Maybe you think I'm angry, but I'm not."

The look in her eyes told Allan otherwise. That look had long since replaced furtive glances of desire. He knew that look too well.

"I've taken care of you for the last two weeks,"

she continued. "I did not do it because I am your wife. I didn't feel obligated or required. I did it because I wanted to. Do you know how easy it would have been for me to take the kids and leave you with Mr. Zook?"

Allan interrupted, "Who's Mr. Zook?" He hoped the question would derail her rant.

"What? It's Ben Abrim," she answered. Allan never thought to ask him. Tina continued, "That's right, I talked to him. He told me what would be expected of you now, what would be expected of us."

"It's something we can do, right?" hoped Allan.

"That's what I've been thinking about. I've seen a change in you in the past month, since that night we took the kids Christmas shopping. I haven't seen this kind of passion in you since our honeymoon. Coming here, I barely know you. But I do know this, you have strength. You know you probably had pneumonia?" said Tina.

Allan shifted uncomfortably on the seat facing his wife. Deep down in his gut, he could feel it tightening. They say that females have a sixth sense, women's intuition, but Allan understood now that men have it too. He already knew to what his wife was leading and he did not want to hear it.

"I knew I was sick. I knew you were there to take care of me," he said.

"Is that enough?" she asked. "I've had plenty of alone time with the kids working over at the Menlachs. I think Alice is starting to like it here.

But my point is that I'm not mad. I've made a few decisions from a place of peace. That's what Mr. Zook said praying is all about. So, I prayed. I don't know what your beliefs are now, but I think they are very different from mine. I can see that you have a purpose here. I won't take that away from you. I won't stand in your way."

The tightness in Allan's chest became unbearable. He wanted her to say it and be done.

Tina said, "We used to be friends once. Best friends. I want that back, but I don't think we can do that as husband and wife."

Allan knew that would be as close as she would come to saying the d-word. He asked himself if he wanted a divorce. He had asked that question too many times over the years and way too many in the past year. He believed he wanted to stay together. He believed coming here would fix their relationship.

Somewhere behind throbbing temples and under a racing pulse, Allan heard that comforting voice again, "Set her free."

Allan suddenly realized that being set free could mean something different for Tina than it did for him. He thought moving to Karsten Field meant they could fix their relationship and stay together. A totally new thought occurred to him that being apart might fix their relationship.

The idea contradicted everything he thought he'd been fighting for. If he came here only for their marriage to end, then why did he come here, he asked himself. They could have stayed in Des Moines and gotten a divorce there. Then Allan concentrated on the words *set her free*. Those words loosened his chest and untied his stomach.

Before he could tell her any of his thoughts, Tina said, "I went looking for a phone a couple days ago. Whatever becomes of us, I can't stay here. My mom has been diagnosed with Alzheimer's. It's not bad yet, but she is going to need somebody to take care of her. Apparently, I'm pretty good at taking care of other people."

Tina's mother had always been good to them. She never fell into any of those Mother-in-Law stereotypes and Allan had a good relationship with her. It became clear that he needed to set Tina free for that purpose alone. He knew Tina would stay with her mother to the end and treat her right.

Allan stood up and pulled Tina to her feet. He wrapped his arms around her tightly and she squeezed back. Both of them wept silently, partly out of sorrow for what was gone and partly for relief of what was to come. Allan struggled to push out a few more words, "I guess this is a new beginning."

Learning

At his mother's request, Brett spent a lot of time at the Menlach home. When he saw his father carried into the house two weeks ago, he understood the man in a new way. Being fourteen, he thought of himself as an adult, but that night was the first time he saw the world with adult eyes.

Brett thought he understood what his father had done. He really did not know much about sacrifice or commitment. He was not exactly sure which his dad did in the river. Either way, it made him feel a little more grown up. With his father sick in bed, it made him feel a little more responsible. With that responsibility came work, hard work.

Brett would gladly travel the World Wide Web. He could battle monsters and save princesses on his Nintendo. Brett tricked himself into thinking he was capable of many things, but they were virtual things. He did not like the outdoors. He did not like animals. Now he had a surplus of both.

Amos Menlach reminded Brett of his own late grandfather. A portly man that liked to laugh, Brett could not resent doing chores for him. The Menlachs had six children and they all participated in the work. As far as little kids go, Brett kind of liked the younger Menlachs. The pre-teen girls, Katie and Annie, did not pester or annoy him like the twelve to fourteen year old girls he knew back at school. They did seem to whisper and giggle quite a lot, but it did not bother him. The seven-year-old twins, Michael and Dolph, had to be the most rambunctious boys Brett had ever seen. Their energy lasted from sunrise to sunset. The young boys helped with some chores, but mostly they played in the snow.

When the snow melted some, they found mud puddles to roll into as well.

The two oldest Menlach children seemed much more serious than the rest of their family combined. Twenty-four year old David took the most responsibility around the farm. He kept the younger kids on task and personally showed Brett how to do the things that needed to be done. Twenty-year-old Samuel did his share of work and still found time to take Brett back to their cabin and make sure things were in order there.

Until coming to Karsten Field, the closest Brett had ever been to a cow was McDonald's. Now he impressed himself by being able to milk one and keep most of it in the bucket. The cow did not seem to mind the highly personal interaction as much as Brett did. He hoped David did not see him blush the first time he put his hand on the warm udder. Nothing on the internet had prepared him for this.

Brett noticed a change in his sister too. She looked to be enjoying herself. Without her iPod, she actually had to participate in conversations. It amazed him to see that his sister actually had some intelligence. He always thought she would end up being a dumb model or some baser profession. Her ability to communicate with Mrs. Menlach and relate to the girls helped Brett feel more like he belonged.

Aside from giving up his electronics, wearing his hat was the hardest thing for Brett. It fit him well, but he felt constricted. The only time he did not mind wearing it was out in the field. It was still too early to start working the topsoil or to do any planting. However, David insisted that they needed to walk the fields and know them so that no time was wasted when the weather turned. He expected more snow in February and March and Brett appreciated the warmth that his hat provided.

The other thing Brett noticed about Alice was how she gave extra attention to the freckle-faced Samuel. Alice always enjoyed the attention of boys, and men once she turned eighteen, but she never had a boyfriend. She used to state that she had a career to think of and did not have time for games. Brett never saw either.

Brett and Alice would have lunch with the whole Menlach family. This was a needed break for Brett as he built up his endurance. Two weeks had yet to beat years of keyboard jockeying. By no means overweight, Brett simply did not have the stamina for such a dramatic change in lifestyle. So he looked forward to lunch. Somehow, Alice always managed to be seated next to or directly across from Samuel.

She did not confide in him and Brett saw no advances on her part. He guessed she did not want to offend anyone. He thought Mrs. Menlach might be quite scary if someone upset her. Still, he did notice the occasional furtive glance from Samuel. They barely even spoke to each other, but those glances were there.

Igniting

Two days before Allan got out of bed, Brett finished his chores in record time. He understood that his new friends were not focused on physical rewards, but he felt like he deserved something for the accomplishment. That night, Brett easily found the key to the storage shed that held all their possessions. He lifted it quietly out of the drawer as his father slept.

Brett felt like he should get to do something he enjoyed. He had been doing things for everybody else for almost two weeks straight. He missed his old life of solitude. He wanted to find a quiet spot where he could be alone. After David showed him how clean and organized the Menlach barn was, Samuel took Brett to their barn. No one in his family had been in their barn yet. The wooden door creaked open on its ancient-looking hinges. There amidst the clutter and disrepair, so close to his new home, Brett found his spot.

Samuel did not pay much attention to the barn, but he specifically pointed out one thing. In the corner of the last stall, covered by a dusty tarp, Samuel revealed a large, square generator.

"I didn't think you guys used electricity?" said Brett.

"We don't," said Samuel in a hushed tone. He looked in awe of the outdated machine. "Mr. Tunstile sometimes had need of it. We were never allowed to visit at the times when the long orange cord stretched from the barn to the cabin."

"Does it still work?" asked Brett. He looked at the bank of dials and row of outlets across the front. He had already started formulating his own plan.

"I should think not," Samuel said as he draped the tarp over the tempting box.

Once Brett had his father's key, he got up early the next day and snuck down to the Emporium. This collection of shops and restaurants reminded him of something from the TV show Fringe or maybe a J.J. Abrams movie. Covering the three miles in the early morning light felt like enough of an accomplishment deserving of his anticipated reward.

When he pushed up the door, he expected to find their things in a broken pile. Instead, someone had taken the time to nicely stack everything. This made it easy for Brett to find his Nintendo DSi. He knew the battery would be drained by now, so he took a few minutes to locate the charger. A tingle of excitement told him his plan was coming to fruition. Brett locked the door and made it back to the cabin before anyone else got out of bed.

On the day Allan had his heart-wrenching talk with Tina; Brett did not go to the Menlachs. He walked out the front door, leaving his mom with the impression that he was off to do chores. Before they crested the first hill, he told Alice that he did not feel well, probably because he shared the bedroom with their dad. Alice continued on and Brett headed back toward the cabin.

Instead of going inside, he hurried around to the barn. He quietly closed the large door and raced to the back corner. Brett had not felt this kind of excitement or anticipation since the last Christmas before Bobby Hanshaw told him a troubling story about Santa Claus. Brett snatched off the tarp, tearing the side on the metal edge.

"I deserve this," he repeated over and over in his head.

He believed one morning of video games would not affect anybody. He had been working hard. He gave up a lot. He deserved some small reward.

The fuel gauge indicated an adequate supply as best as Brett could tell. He saw a few other switches that did not mean anything to him, so he skipped to the start button. He pressed it once.

Nothing.

Nothing?

"C'mon, start," he said aloud.

Brett jammed in the start button again. This time he held it in until he heard a mechanical cough. The generator sputtered to life and belched out a small cloud of black smoke. It dissipated into the rafters like any guilt Brett felt for being in the barn. He let the engine run for a minute while he untangled his charging cord. Then he deliberately plugged it in and watched the light on the back of the DSi begin to glow. It started charging the battery.

He balanced his handheld device on the wall that divided the stalls and then went to the front of the barn to see if his mother noticed any of the noise. While he had his back turned, Brett did not notice the sparks popping out of the long unused outlets. A small fire instantly spread over the dry hay and torn canvas tarp.

When Brett turned back to see the mess he'd created, he started to panic. First, he tried to grab his Nintendo, but only succeeded in knocking it down into the growing flames surrounding the generator.

So far, the fire remained in the four-foot wide stall and Brett thought he could contain it. He saw a bucket full of water and rushed it toward the fire. As he tossed the contents toward the blaze, he noticed the hand scrawled label *Turpentine*. The sudden flash knocked Brett backwards.

From the ground, he watched the hungry flames climb up the back wall like a hand clawing its way out of a grave in one of his horror movies. He said, "Who keeps turpentine in a bucket?"

A rattling noise from the engulfed corner warned Brett of the next danger. He knew it could only be a matter of moments before the fuel inside the generator ignited. He scrambled toward the front of the barn.

Outside, he could hear Samuel yelling, "Fire! Fire!" The older boy must have come looking for Brett when he did not arrive with Alice.

Brett swung open the large front door as the generator exploded. The burst of pressure sent him flailing face first into melting snow and mud. Samuel made it to him and dragged him away from the barn. By then, Allan and Tina joined them as they watched the old wood creak and collapse as the flames consumed it.

Later that evening, several families gathered to observe the damage. Nothing remained of the barn except for smoldering timbers. Brett felt lucky that the flames did not spread to the nearby trees. He had never heard of a forest fire in winter, but did not want to be the cause of it. Brett saw Mr. Zook talking with his father.

"Now I see it is a good thing that I kept Mr. Tunstile's cows in my barn," said Ben Abrim. "Do not worry my friend. These folks here, and a few more I expect, will be glad to help. It has been a while since our last barn raising. When the weather turns, you will see how Karsten Field takes care of its own."

"Thank you," said Allan. "I don't understand how the fire started though."

Ben Abrim looked directly at Brett. The old man's stare bore into him and he felt compelled to tell the truth. He knew he made a huge mistake and confession was the only answer.

Ben Abrim said to Allan, "I think you will understand shortly."

Then the other Karsten families departed for their homes as the sun began to set. The Howarth family walked up the stairs of their cabin. Brett straightened the brim of his hat. He did not look forward to what would come next, but he had to tell his family what he had done.

Chapter Four

Lost Son Found

Smoking

Allan stood on the corner of his front porch. The warmth of last night's barn fire warmed him against the cool morning air. He watched an occasional rill of smoke escape from the smoldering ruins. As the swirling puff reached the top of the nearby trees, it blended in with the dark clouds. Allan imagined his thoughts rising on the smoke. For the moment, he forgot about everything else and poured his heart into that smoke. It suddenly made sense to him that his thoughts could be lifted on that rising heat straight up to God.

"I hope you get this," started Allan. He never really prayed before and definitely never out loud. Somehow, this felt right. "Thank you for keeping my son safe from that fire." He wanted to say more, but the lump in his throat prevented it.

"Good morgen, Mr. Howarth."

The sound of Ben Abrim's voice forced Allan to regain his composure. Allan greeted his friend with a slight well of tears in his eyes.

"Good morning to you, Mr. Zook," said Allan. The short man had a gentle nature that instantly put Allan at ease. Allan asked, "What brings you over so early?"

Making his way onto the porch, Ben Abrim removed his hat. He had a look on his face that Allan guessed to be somewhere between embarrassment and worry.

Ben Abrim said, "Forgive me, if I'm intruding."

"Not at all," started Allan.

"No, I mean forgive me if I'm intruding into your personal affairs. During my morning prayers, I could only think about you and what has happened since you arrived in Karsten Field," said Ben Abrim.

Allan understood exactly what his friend meant. They had not received an overly warm welcome, and then he got pneumonia. Now with the barn incident, most of the other families also knew about him and Tina separating. David, the oldest of the Menlach children, offered his sled to help Tina get her things from storage. That's how Allan ended up alone this morning. Tina, Brett and David went to the storage shed, while Alice decided to go help Mrs. Menlach with breakfast and morning chores.

"To tell you the truth, if you have a good word for me, I could definitely use it," said Allan.

He escorted his friend into the house. Since

everybody had left the cabin, Allan did not bother lighting any candles. With the coming rain clouds, the inside of the cabin looked a little dreary. The dark room seemed to be a perfect metaphor for how Allan felt. He needed a light in his soul to help him cope with his wife's leaving. Because he understood her reasons did not mean he had to like them.

As Allan lit a small candle on the table, Ben Abrim pulled out chairs for both of them. He took his seat, placed his hat on the table and folded his hands over it. Ben Abrim looked to be saying a silent prayer, so Allan sat next to him and waited.

Finally, Ben Abrim raised his head and said, "I think I should share with you the story of Isaac Karsten."

Thunder punctuated his sentence. A long, low rumble came over them and gently shook the cabin. Allan wondered if the thunder meant to keep Ben Abrim from talking or if it bellowed in support of his story. The sound of rain tapping on the roof replaced the thunder. Allan thought about how the rain would squelch the last of the cinders in his former barn. If it kept up for long, he guessed it might melt away any lingering snow. Even though it was only February, it started to feel like spring. Then Allan realized that Tina and Brett would be caught out in the rain. He hoped they would get their things into the car before anything got ruined.

Ben Abrim cleared his throat. He said, "Shall I start at the beginning then?"

Storytelling

In one of the years immediately following the turn of the century, Hezekiah Karsten moved away from his friends in the east. His reasons were his own. Not common of his people, the man struck out on his own, accompanied only by his trusted wife and newborn son.

In those days, Englisher companies did not have the reputation which they do now. Hezekiah found some land and shook hands with the Englisher that owned it. He called the place Thuisland and before long, other families joined Mr. Karsten. Here, Mr. Karsten, with the help of his neighbors, built for himself the house now occupied by Elder Tibold and the very same school that is now standing.

It was in June of 1917, that Isaac Karsten, the only son of Hezekiah and Mary Agnes Karsten turned eighteen years of age. The boy took rumspringa the summer before and believed he had found a calling. Eighteen is no special age for we Amish, but Isaac knew it to be a significant age for the United States government.

Isaac announced his decision to his father that he would join the United States military in the war to protect democracy. Hezekiah sternly reminded Isaac that taking up arms went against the core of their beliefs. Hezekiah prayed that Isaac would come to the understanding that violence was not their way and that he had no part in the affairs of the outside world.

Hezekiah's prayers did not change Isaac's mind. Isaac spoke only of virtue and honor. The boy thought himself a man and believed God showed him a path to help his fellow man. Isaac left home without his parents' permission and winter came to Thuisland.

Isaac's mother worried that her son would be warm and safe with the cold winters of Europe. She could not let her heart fall on the thoughts of her son fighting and killing other human beings.

While Isaac wore his uniform, some changes came to Thuisland. Our first schoolteacher, Rachel Miller lost her husband to bronchitis. When school resumed in February, not only would she have her own newborn child, but also ten young students. Another thought for concern came from Simon Lengacher, Isaac's longtime friend.

As children, Isaac and Simon had been inseparable. They took rumspringa together. However, while Isaac learned to dance the jitterbug, Simon studied art and visited museums. Simon did not condemn Isaacs's decision to join the army as the elders did. Simon had his own challenge. He seemed to have a tendency toward being a painter. Within the confines and under the Ordnung of Thuisland, Simon could not act on his urges to create.

With the coming of spring in the year nineteen-eighteen, so came Isaac Karsten. Despite the perceived horrors of war, most everyone commented that Isaac looked younger and more vibrant than when he left. Everyone thanked God for his return. No one shunned the boy, as he accepted God and received baptism performed by his own father.

Upon his return, Isaac helped with many repairs on the Karsten farm. Hezekiah had become too old already to do some of the heaviest labor. While Simon remained a good friend, he had to help with his family's farm and help in raising his three younger brothers. In those few weeks, Isaac worked to make God proud. Every task, he completed with a smile.

In his spare time, several wives noticed Isaac spending time with the widowed schoolteacher, Rachel Miller. No one imagined the younger man courting the widow. Isaac stayed very public in his actions as he helped with Ms. Miller's baby and did chores, like whitewashing the schoolhouse.

Those same wives that saw Isaac with Rachel also noticed a change in the schoolteacher. It had been said that before Isaac returned, Ms. Miller looked all too forlorn. She had ended school early before winter and spent many isolated hours with her baby. Those that talked suspected she feared her baby would succumb to the same disease to which her husband did. They noticed that Rachel started to slip away from her faith. The week before Isaac returned, she did not attend Sunday prayers or choir. The people of Thuisland worried that Rachel Miller would not open the school this year, as she was already three weeks behind schedule.

Something in Isaac's actions must have rekindled Rachel Miller's faith. With a few days a week helping, Isaac guided Ms. Miller back to her path. Many believe that Ms. Miller would have left the faith altogether had it not been for Isaac Karsten. Over the course of a few weeks, Rachel Miller went from being a recluse to one of the most well known members of Thuisland. She managed to care for her baby, teach school and lead the Sunday choir.

Simon Lengacher shared a similar experience with Isaac. He too had been struggling with his faith, but did not tell his best friend until Isaac had been home for several weeks. Simon confessed to Isaac that he had a longing to paint again. He believed God had blessed him with a talent that should not be hidden. Simon wanted to remain modest, but no one in Thuisland had a need for his ability.

Isaac and Simon spent one afternoon talking about art.

"Realize our parents have built a home here and that their intentions are pure," said Isaac.

"Of course, I have given myself fully to God," said Simon.

"But you are not yet baptized?" asked Isaac.

"What do you mean by that?" replied Simon.

"In your heart, the Lord tells you that you have a different path to walk."

"Do you believe that?" asked Simon.

"I have seen you paint. I have seen the way your art gives glory to God. You would not be one of those artists that partake of the baser acts of the flesh. If you chose to leave the Amish, it would be because God himself presented you with that opportunity. My father believes those who walk a different path will never walk with God. However, I am sure that your paintings will show others the way," explained Isaac.

"By sacrificing my own salvation, I could save many others?" asked Simon.

"By bringing others to God, you will only ensure your salvation," said Isaac.

With those words, Simon decided to give himself to God through art. He left Thuisland the very next morning for New York and art school. He found work as a dishwasher in a Bronx deli and paid his way through art school without a single scholarship.

[At this point, Ben Abrim pauses and points to a painting hanging above the fireplace. The cracked oils on the stretched canvas show a man walking out into a field. There are two sets of footprints leading up to him. Allan had looked at that painting almost every day since moving into the cabin. He notices Simon Lengacher's signature in the lower right corner for the first time. Ben Abrim explains that Mr. Tunstile owned the only painting in Karsten Field created by Mr. Lengacher. Ben Abrim then continues the story of Isaac Karsten.]

In the month of Isaac Karsten's return, people saw only the glory of God in him. That is why they were so shocked when, one morning, he had disappeared. Mary Agnes Karsten prepared breakfast while she thought her husband and son were milking cows and feeding chickens. Hezekiah came into the kitchen from the barn and wondered aloud where Isaac had been that morning. He saw his son's empty bed and surmised that Isaac had gone out early to help one of their neighbors. Mrs. Karsten checked her son's bed and confirmed that the sheets and blanket looked as though no one slept in them last night.

Hezekiah took his buggy down to the schoolhouse, only to find that Ms. Miller had not seen Isaac either. At this time, Thuisland had about as many residents as we do now, and Mr. Karsten felt compelled to call on them all for the whereabouts of his son.

No one that day had seen Isaac Karsten.

Near lunchtime, Hezekiah heard an unfamiliar sound. A dust covered motorcycle roared its way up to the front of his house. The small plate on the back showed that the cyclist had come all the way from Des Moines, the state capitol. The man did not bother to remove his gloves or raise his goggles. He held two pieces of paper and simply said, "Sign here," indicating the paper in his left hand. Hezekiah obliged and then received the paper from the stranger's right hand. The motorcycling deliveryman did not wait for Hezekiah to read the paper. He rode away as fast as he had arrived.

Hezekiah Karsten broke the seal of what turned out to be a telegram. He read:

From: United States Army
To: Parents of Isaac Karsten

Thank you on behalf of US Army STOP Regret to inform Isaac Karsten killed in action six weeks ago STOP

Mr. and Mrs. Karsten could not believe the narrow yellow paper in front of them. If their son had been killed six weeks ago, then who had been sleeping in his bed the last four weeks? Both of them grieved silently wondering who had been helping Rachel Miller at the school and who encouraged the Lengacher boy to follow his dream of painting.

Hezekiah Karsten dropped the telegram and fell to his knees. He raised his open hands to the sky and, with tears in his eyes, said, "Mein Gott, I am your servant and know not my part in your plan. All glory is yours. Please hold my son in your bosom. Forgive him that he took up arms and know that he did it to protect those that could not protect themselves. I bear witness to your miracle and praise you for sharing this blessing. My Isaac has been set free."

"Mr. Karsten showed the telegram to all of his neighbors," said Ben Abrim. "They agreed on that day to change the name of Thuisland to Karsten Field as a tribute to the Lord's miracle."

Allan could not believe the story. At first, he did not want to. He suspected Ben Abrim had only been trying to encourage him or distract him from his worry. Then he realized the lack of God in his own life. For too long, he struggled with work and relationships. Suddenly, everything that changed in his life had to do with God. A new home came from a man that Allan had long forgotten because that man said it was God's plan.

It felt like Allan's heart almost stopped at the words of Karsten's prayer. When Ben Abrim repeated the words *set free*, Allan felt sweat form on his forehead and the palms of his hands. He guessed the color rushed out of his face, but Ben Abrim did not react with concern. However, Allan did not feel distress. The words *set free* had become like a mantra. He kept hearing them over and over, but had not shared them with anybody. Allan felt himself start to swoon. He became completely overwhelmed with the knowledge that God wanted him to be here in Karsten Field.

Packing

Tina did not share the same outlook as her husband. Leading up to this tumultuous turn of events, she did not think she had anything in common with Allan anymore.

They grew apart.

That was a good euphemism. They tried counseling. She even agreed to move with him to the middle of nowhere. She did not think the transplant could be called a success.

Nothing seemed to go right since they moved to Karsten Field. So few of the other families would speak to them. Then Allan got sick. And for the proverbial icing, Brett almost started a forest fire trying to play a video game.

Tina did not try to fool herself. She could see all of Allan's potential. She truly believed he belonged here. Those same observations showed her how much she did not belong. Allan was her best friend, but that did not mean they had to stay married.

Friends grow apart.

Riding on David Menlach's sled only reminded Tina that she did not belong here. The thick wooden runners worked great on the snow. When they hit a patch of mud, the two-horse team could not pull them out of the bog. Luckily, Tina insisted on Brett helping her. The Menlach boy and Brett pushed while she held the reigns. They made it free, but not before the horses splashed Tina repeatedly. Although accidental, it did not make her feel any less muddy.

Their possessions had been neatly stacked. That made it easy for Tina to sort out what she would leave behind in the storage shed. She had no use for Allan's Blu-Ray player or golf clubs. As she prepared the first of her boxes, it started raining. Tina took it as another sign that she was not supposed to be here.

David went to the next storage shed and came back with a large plastic sheet. He covered the first box on his sled and unfolded the plastic to cover the rest of what they would load.

After carrying his third box, Brett stopped and said, "Let me come with you."

The request did not completely surprise Tina. She knew Brett was having a hard time adjusting.

He did not have the same reasons for staying that his sister did. Tina noticed a change in Alice.

"I'm going to live with Gram," Tina said.

"I know. I can help you," said Brett. "Besides, it's still in the same school district. I would be back with my friends."

Tina could not bring herself to say yes. She felt like she would be tearing her family in half.

Instead, she said, "What about your father?"

She watched anger and some other emotion flash across Brett's face. Could he be old enough to feel indignation, she wondered.

Brett said, "He didn't ask me to come here. Why do I have to ask him to leave? I'm almost fifteen, not a little kid."

"I don't know what to say," started Tina. She really did not know. Other than the feeling that Allan belonged here, she had no other reason why Brett could not come with her.

"I understand better than you think," said Brett. "I've seen the change in him. It's like he woke up, if that makes sense?"

It did make sense to Tina. She felt the same way, like she had been asleep. Or more like she had been sleepwalking. This move snapped them out of it. Waking up helped Tina see things more clearly. Maybe, she allowed, Brett and Alice also shared a new understanding.

Tina thought for a moment about her children as children. When they were little, Alice always followed her father. Brett typically ended up in her lap, always his mama's boy. Somehow, this split seemed natural, justifiable.

"Moving back to Des Moines won't make me stop being his son. I respect his decision, but I don't fit here," said Brett.

Tina looked at her son, standing in the rain. He looked like her little boy, but his eyes showed the sincerity of an adult. She pulled wet strands of hair out of her face. David Menlach coughed, either as a reminder of his presence or the rain getting to him. Apparently, he did not know what to put on the sled next and had been waiting on her.

"Oh," said Tina. "Sorry, David. Brett, let's get your things. I'll talk to your father."

Brett gave her a reassuring smile. It showed strength that she never expected from any fourteen year old. He said, "It's okay. I'll tell him."

Ending

That afternoon, they ate their last meal together as a family. Tina made sandwiches while Allan listened to his son. Brett's directness and certainty impressed Allan. He had not expected his son to act so maturely.

During the course of their lunch, Alice announced, "I am staying."

"I thought you would," said Tina. "I knew you had a reason to."

"Mom, please," said Alice. Allan had not seen his daughter blush like this since she won the fifth grade science fair. Something unsaid passed between Alice and her mother, but Allan had no idea what. Whatever her reason for staying, he did not think it had anything to do with him.

Allan watched his wife save his daughter by changing the subject. She said, "We've got the car loaded. If we leave as soon as we're done eating, I can be to my mom's before dark."

The conversation turned to Tina's mother's health and then to Brett's school. For the first time in a long time, the four of them sat, talked and laughed in a way that Allan did not recognize. On the last day of being together, they had finally become a real family. Allan hated that they were separating. However, he understood that they all needed to be free, not only him.

After lunch, Brett and Alice waited outside with Ben Abrim and the Menlach family. Allan shared one last private moment with his wife. His brain reminded him that she would soon be his ex-wife. He held her in his arms, feeling love, but not as a husband and wife. Allan did not think it would make him feel any better, but he wanted to tell her something that Ben Abrim told him that morning.

"Mr. Zook said something interesting about our marriage," said Allan.

"He always has something interesting to say," added Tina. "I like that little man."

"Me too." Allan choked back an urge to cry. He said, "He said that since I was baptized and you weren't then they don't recognize our marriage. Actually, it's like we were never married. If you decide to do the paperwork, our divorce would only be a formality. Once you leave here, I basically start with a blank slate."

"Does that make you happy?" asked Tina.

"That's not fair," said Allan. "I am not happy to lose you. That is the reason I came here in the first place. Now I understand that God has other plans for me. I feel closer to Him in Karsten Field. When you make a life without me, then I will know that I did the right thing by letting you go."

Both Allan and Tina began crying. They held each other tightly and let out silent, heavy sobs. Years of frustration, jealousy, and anger fell out of them in those sobs. Allan reflected on their twenty-two years of marriage. He realized now that, for too long, they stayed together although they had nothing between them. He fought so hard to keep them together because he was scared of what it might be like not being together.

Now, Allan felt like he was standing on a high cliff. Had they gone through this divorce back in Des Moines, he surely would have fallen off that cliff. Being where he was now and feeling how he felt, once Tina let go of him, Allan felt like he would fly from that cliff and soar through the sky.

He thought he saw a change in Tina, as well. He hoped and believed her life would be better without him. He always thought she was the strong one in their relationship. He knew she would come through this experience stronger.

Finally, Tina spoke. She said, "I've seen signs too. You're not the only one talking to God. He has shown me plenty of reasons for leaving, like you getting sick. Even this morning, the sled got stuck in the mud."

Allan said, "Do you think those might possibly be signs to stay. Maybe He is trying to block your path."

"I thought about that, but too many unfortunate things keep happening," Tina said. "I know in my heart that as soon as I am gone, something wonderful will happen for you."

Beginning

Ben Abrim arrived at six in the morning the day after Tina and Brett left. Alice already made a small breakfast for her father and left to work with Sarah Menlach. Ben Abrim waited while Allan finished eating.

Today, Allan felt achy and not quite used to getting up before the sun. He knew it would not be long before he started having to worry about his field. He believed that hard work would be his next spiritual obstacle. He also realized that he had committed himself to the school and today would be the first day of that adventure.

"Ms. Reece started classes last week. She always gives the children a long winter break. I wanted to make sure you were recovered before I showed you to the school," said Ben Abrim.

"You know I am not a teacher," said Allan.

"Before a couple weeks ago, you were not

Amish either," said Ben Abrim with a smile.

"I'm not that either."

"Not yet, but everybody's path is different," said Ben Abrim.

The rain had melted much of the snow, so Allan rode with Ben Abrim in his two-wheeled buggy. The wooden wheels looked sturdy and had no problem handling the mud. They rode close to the business area where tourists could get a glimpse of their private community. Then Ben Abrim guided the horses slightly to the northwest.

The school did not look any different from the surrounding houses. Allan wondered if it was the same school started by Rachel Miller so many years ago. She must have converted her house into the school.

As they rolled to a stop in front of the school, Ben Abrim began explaining, "You have twenty students from nine different families: the Fencils; Menlachs, who you know; more Fencils, Elder Tibold's grandchildren; one Miller; two Otto families; Gundy; Kurtz and Troyer. I do not expect you will remember all of their names on the first day.

They made their way up the front stairs. Ben Abrim stomped the mud out of the treads of his heavy boots. Allan tried scraping his shoes.

"I will show you Mr. Tunstile's old office. I am sure you will make it your own. Beyond that, I will leave it to Ms. Reece to show you the rest of the school. She is, after all, the teacher."

Ben Abrim did as he said. He led Allan to a cluttered office stacked with books that seemed to be more about the outside world than the Amish world. Ben Abrim looked satisfied. He nodded to Allan and then left. Allan leafed through a few papers on the desk, not knowing what he might find. Then he decided to meet the students and teacher.

Allan walked from the office down a short hall to a large room. It looked to be a living room converted to a classroom. Twenty children filled every desk. Two of the youngest had to share one desk. Allan had never seen such a quiet classroom. Not one of the students made a sound and no one looked up at him as he entered the room.

Standing by the chalkboard, Allan saw something else he never expected. The teacher wore a long blue dress that covered her arms and ran down to her ankles. A hand-knitted kapp covered her close-cropped brown hair, hanging barely below her earlobes. She had smooth white skin dotted with a small patch of freckles on each cheek.

When Mary Reece glanced at him, Allan thought he saw a sparkle in her cool brown eyes. She nodded to him and Allan nodded back.

"The children are reading scripture," said Ms. Reece, with no other greeting.

Allan replied, "That sounds wonderful."

CHAPTER FIVE

THE BLUE DOOR

School Work

Allan discovered that his duties at the school did not all pertain to teaching. After the passing of his old teacher, Ms. Reece started keeping a list of chores that needed completion. She plainly and directly lined out these chores to Allan.

Without argument, Allan went to work. Melting snow showed him a few places where the roof needed patching. Of course, spring meant a new whitewash for the outside of the schoolhouse. At first, Allan found the manual labor to be exhilarating. He had not quite gained his full strength back from the pneumonia and decided this would be a good way to do it. Allan did not have much knowledge in painting or roofing, but he did not want to disappoint Ms. Reece or the memory of Shepherd Tunstile.

From the roof of the schoolhouse, Allan could see the business street that he once referred to as a scene from the Twilight Zone. After three months of living in Karsten Field, he understood it a little better. That street, with its shops and two restaurants existed as Karsten Field's connection to the outside world. Not only did it generate money, which even the Amish needed, but also it acted as a buffer to keep their private lives private.

In addition to the fantastic view, Allan got more than his share of splinters from the hand-cut wood shingles. That did not keep him from pouring the sticky resin and wedging the replacement shingles into their necessary spots. The practical design of the slightly pitched roof meant that Allan did not have to be perfect in his repair work. He realized that all he had to do was cover the major holes, then God and physics would do the rest.

His good friend Ben Abrim stopped for a visit after Allan had been working a few days. The older man wanted to make sure that he was getting settled. He also brought him a ham sandwich made from the pig Isaac Gundy slaughtered only a week ago. Ben Abrim must have noticed how gingerly Allan held the fresh baked bread. The small, smiling man said, "Sore hands make a strong heart." Then he handed over a pair of work gloves that Allan could have used two days before. Ben Abrim added, "God favors the prepared." Allan had grown to enjoy his friend's *little sayings*.

One cool morning, Ms. Reece asked Allan to chop wood for their stoves.

"Being that it is not yet spring, the school house does tend to keep a chill," explained the schoolteacher, Mary Reece. "Please see to it that we keep the rooms warm. Understand, this is not for me, but the children become distracted when they are cold."

Despite her assurance, Allan suspected the fire would be for her as well. She seemed proud and wanted to show her fortitude, not only to the children, but to him too.

Allan did not know what to make of Mary Reece. She looked young, probably ten years younger than himself. However, she seemed mature and maybe a little stern. She kept control of her classroom. Allan saw disciplined children unlike he never encountered the few times he visited Brett or Alice's schools. It seemed that Ms. Reece wanted Karsten Field to perceive her as independent and resilient. After her husband died, she apparently did not even entertain the idea of remarrying.

Between chores, Ms. Reece invited Allan into the classroom. She explained that Mr. Tunstile had taught math and some biology of the farm animals. Allan did not think he could teach algebra or any advanced concepts. He told her he knew very little of biology.

"Addition and subtraction will suffice," said Ms. Reece. "At their age, they are not expected to do more than count bushels or number rows in the field."

It occurred to Allan that these children would probably never have to worry about mortgage rates or computer programming. He believed he could teach them the basic concepts that would be used in their small town.

The enrolled students consisted of twenty children from ages five to fifteen. They shared the same classroom and studied the same topics. The older students came to school later, as they were expected to complete morning chores at home first. Some of the older ones came early because they were responsible for bringing their younger siblings, like the Menlachs and Fencils.

Because Allan did not spend too much time with the kids yet, he had a difficult time learning names. He shared many meals with the Menlach family, so he knew their children well enough. Being two sets of twins, he could not tell Annie from Katie or Michael from Dolph, however. Elder Tibold Fencil had eight children, four of which came to school. Elder Tibold's oldest son, Matthew, had a family of his own and three school age children.

The two youngest boys, Malachi Miller and Simon Otto, seemed to be inseparable. They arrived together and left together, accompanied either by Mrs. Miller or Mrs. Otto. They even shared the same bible for their reading lessons.

Allan felt like the children responded to him well enough. They seemed to like him. That made it easier for Allan to adjust to his new calling. He did not know if he would be able to relate to the children. It felt like such a long time since his own had been small and less independent. Most of his previous work life had been spent communicating with adults.

Ms. Reece suggested, "Treat them as adults. The world will expect them to act as such soon enough. If you treat them like children, then they will act like children. They deserve as much respect as you would like in return."

It surprised him the day Ethel Kurtz gave him a hug. The seven-year-old girl said, "I'm glad you're my teacher." Then, she skipped out of the classroom. After that, none of the students left the school without giving Allan a farewell in the form of a hug or handshake in the same way that they did with Ms. Reece every day. Little Ethel made Allan feel like he truly belonged in Karsten Field for the first time.

Over the next several weeks, Allan paid a great deal of attention to Mary Reece. He felt that she had a lot to offer on the subject of being a teacher. He wanted to learn from her because he felt a need to give as much as he could to the people of Karsten Field. He could not put it clearly into words, but he knew he was supposed to be here and the families had opened their doors and hearts to him and Alice.

One afternoon, Allan entered the classroom after the students had left. He wanted nothing more than some advice on dealing with the children. He found Ms. Reece sitting at her desk, engrossed in an unidentifiable book.

It surprised him when Ms. Reece said, "Mr. Howarth, I do not think it is appropriate for us to be alone together."

Allan looked around in shock. Her statement made him feel self-conscious and strangely guilty.

He wondered what in his behavior caused her to respond in such a way.

"I apologize if I offended you in some way," he said.

"No offence at all," said Ms. Reece. "It is only that we are both single adults. I would not want anyone to think you are courting me when you are not."

Courting? Allan understood exactly what she meant and it was the last thought on his mind. His wife of twenty-two years left him, amicably enough, only a few weeks ago. The last thing he could imagine would be starting a new relationship or courting anyone. In the brief moment that Allan took to process this, he also looked at Ms. Reece in a new way. He saw a beautiful woman hidden beneath her kapp and a tightly pulled bun of hair. She looked strong and intelligent and he knew she was capable. An idea flashed in his mind like the sudden combustion of a grease fire on his stove. He did not think it would be out of the question that they could be courting. The heat from that imagined fire flushed Allan's cheeks red. As easily as he conceived of it, Allan forced the idea out of his mind. He did not want to entertain such thoughts and doubted if Ms. Mary Reece had an inkling of similar feelings.

"I completely understand," Allan finally said. "I would not want anyone to mistake our acquaintance for anything else. Please, if you have any other tasks, leave a list on my desk for Monday morning."

Mary Reece nodded and turned her attention back to the book on her desk. Allan left the school with a vague, nagging confusion.

Home Work

Allan's duties at the school served as an excuse for not doing his chores at home. Alice spent most of her time with Sarah Menlach and her twins, Katie and Annie. Neither he nor Alice spent much time at home, which meant there was not much that needed doing.

The only real chore Allan had was cleaning the debris from the burned barn. Consequently, he spent his Saturdays and Sundays doing that. The daunting task made Allan greatly wish he had his old power tools. As it was, he borrowed a handsaw and hammer from Ben Abrim. Most of the big rafters did not burn to ash, so Allan had to cut the beams down to carryable lengths. In the time it took to cut through one piece with the handsaw, he knew he could have cut the entire beam with a chainsaw.

Allan found one bright spot in the blackened remains. From one Saturday to the next, he could cut through the beams faster. It occurred to him that he had not felt his upper arms so toned since he was in his mid-twenties. Maybe he could have finished the clean-up job already with power tools, but at what other cost? He admitted to himself that he did not consider all of the benefits or drawbacks of changing his lifestyle. Improving his health came as a surprise.

He took a deep, clear breath and went back to the charred wood. Allan refused offers of help from the older Menlach boys. Although he did not start the fire, Allan felt responsible. Brett would never have been in there had Allan not forced him to come. He realized how foolish it might have seemed that he suddenly made such a drastic change. Clearly, it did not work for his wife or son and he never could have predicted how it worked for his daughter. Allan knew he had to accept everything that came to him along this path. This philosophy made him view the barn debris as a task of his soul in addition to his body.

He would clear the wood by himself.

Luke Lenaxel, the man with the second most children in Karsten Field, stopped by to offer his help one Saturday. After listening to Allan's reason for working alone, Mr. Lenaxel had one suggestion. If Allan would burn the remaining wood, Mr. Lenaxel would take the ash for his compost. He also would make sure the other men knew and he did not doubt they would haul the ash away as well. Family by family, Allan finally met all of the fathers and eldest sons of Karsten Field. Even Elder Tibold's oldest son Matthew came by with his wife, Barbara, and their three daughters. Allan recognized Eartha, Dortha and Martha as his students, but did not make the connection that they were Elder Tibold's granddaughters until Matthew mentioned his father.

"I must tell you that my father has not

officially stopped shunning you," said Matthew. "I do not think he would admit it outside of his own parlor, but I think he likes what you have been doing."

"That means a lot," said Allan.

"When he does the spring baptisms, I have a feeling he would like to see you and your daughter there," said Matthew.

"But I have been baptized."

Matthew ran four fingers through his reddish beard, like a rake through tiny, tangled vines. He explained, "It is customary that the Elder performs the baptisms. Besides, it would give you the opportunity to recite the Dordrecht."

Allan felt his face go white and he knew Matthew had to see it too. He could not believe that they would want him to recite the Dordrecht Confession. It was one of the articles that Ben Abrim gave him to read while he convalesced. Regrettably, Allan had not consciously thought of it since then, with the exception of seeing some of his older students studying it. He understood it to be the basis of their faith and, as such, the basis of his new faith. Still, privately, he thought his faith had grown, and would continue, through his actions and relations.

"Oh, when will that be?" Allan almost stammered.

"In two weeks, church will be at my father's house. The river should be warm enough by then. This time you can take your hat off before you get in the water," chuckled Matthew.

Allan went back to work, practically dreading

the future. He had no problem with public speaking, but he sincerely doubted he could memorize the entire Confession in that short of time. Anybody else that would be getting baptized would have been studying the Dordrecht for years. Worse still, he had no idea if Alice had read it or even heard of it. Luckily, the worries passed with the arrival of Ben Abrim Zook.

The jovial, old man chose to walk today and Allan could see him coming down the hill from almost a mile away. Eventually, Ben Abrim came close enough that Allan dropped his gloves and walked toward him to close the distance. He let out his angst in a brief explanation.

Ben Abrim simply said, "If it is His plan, you will do it."

The clarity of that idea shocked Allan. He believed God had a plan. He believed that plan for him was moving to Karsten Field. In those few short words from Ben Abrim, Allan suddenly had a new understanding. *If it is His plan, you will do it.* That did not only apply to memorizing the Confession, but to everything. Absolutely, totally and completely everything. For the first time in his life, Allan understood that nothing was set before him that was not part of God's plan. Through everything good or bad, God would carry him and deliver him to where he was supposed to be, not according to any human plan, but His own. He believed the words he previously heard. *Set Free.* Now, he understood those words with a new dimension. He was not only set free from a few unpleasant things in his old life, but also set free from all worry and doubt.

This realization came over Allan quickly and settled into his heart and the back of his mind. He knew he could not instantly change his entire way of thinking as easily as he drove down the highway to come here. Maybe he had an epiphany, but he knew his change would not happen overnight. He suspected it could take years. He felt relief that, at least, he had a starting point.

"I have only known you a few months, Mr. Zook, but you are a good friend," said Allan. "I want to thank you for being a part of my life."

Ben Abrim smiled his face-stretching smile. Everyone that knew the old man only ever thought of him like this. His smile conveyed everything in his heart. Only goodness and kindness shone out of that smile. Even strangers that came to the shops of Karsten Field became like friends at the sight of his beaming face.

"Mr. Howarth, I have told you before that God has crossed our paths. How can I not be pleased by something that the Lord has set before me?" said Ben Abrim. "Now, to the reason for my visit. Tomorrow, it is my turn to host church. It is about time that you join us." Ben Abrim put his hands on his hips and silently surveyed the remains of Allan's barn.

"I thought Elder Tibold had church at his house. I assumed I wasn't invited," said Allan.

Ben Abrim picked at the splinters on the top of the waist high beam that used to be a doorpost. He said, "We have church every other Sunday and each member takes a turn of inviting the other members into their home. In two weeks, it will be Mr. Fencil's turn. Tomorrow, it is at my home and you are always welcome there. I understand you have met the Karsten men and know many of their children. You have no excuse not to meet the rest of your new brothers and sisters."

It seemed like a good idea. Allan believed he should know everyone considering he had lived here about three months and there were only fourteen families. He graciously accepted Ben Abrim's invitation.

At the end of the day, Allan looked at the wreckage of his barn and discovered it was now more bare earth than burned wood. He had cleared enough charred timber that he could see the end of his task. He guessed maybe he had two or three more solid days of work. The only thing he could not figure out how to move was the cumbersome generator that caused the whole mess. He decided that he would not worry about that since the sun was already dropping below the tree line.

Social Work

After another Saturday learning to quilt with Mrs. Menlach, Alice came home with dinner. Still warm, Allan ate everything on the plate. With each bite, he thanked God for Sarah Menlach's talents in the kitchen. He understood why Amos Menlach had such a large belly.

Between bites, Allan tried to think of a way to ask Alice to go to church with him. They never went to any kind of church back in Des Moines. He had been getting along so well with his daughter that he did not want to incite an argument.

"Why don't you go to church with me in the morning?" he suggested. Allan ended up using the direct approach. He braced for a possible backlash.

Instead of a complaint, Alice said, "Okay."

Okay? Allan could not believe his ears. No disputes. No snide comments. He understood that he was not the only one making changes in their new life.

He had to double check, "It is all day, you know. That's not a problem for you?"

Alice tried to hide a smile. "I think it will be good for both of us."

She did not offer anything else. Allan did not know what to make of that smile. He suspected his daughter might have some other reason for wanting to go to church. He thought back to the hints of a conversation between Alice and her mother. Almost from the beginning, Alice seemed to want to be here. She found something that made it easy to accept her new life. Maybe, Allan thought, he was the stereotypical oblivious father, but he could not quite figure out what her mysterious reason was.

In the morning, Allan solved the mystery.

Samuel Menlach, the second oldest of the Menlach children, arrived in front of their house in a two-wheeled buggy pulled by a chestnut horse. It's brushed, black tail hung almost to the ground. Allan came down his front steps to say good morning to the young man. He assumed Samuel would be taking them to Ben Abrim's house. That is when he saw the buggy only had room for two on the bench.

The realization punched Allan in the stomach. His breath left and his knees unlocked like they had done only a few times in his life. After the absurd parade of boyfriends Alice had in high school, she had found one of which her father would approve. He had to. This terrified him.

He hoped Alice had wanted to stay with him for countless other reasons. None of them included her falling in love. Allan did not have to ask her. He felt it now. Although it scared him, he accepted it. He wanted her to be happy and free. He did not think he was ready to lose his little girl. However, at eighteen, he had to be kidding himself that she was still little.

When Alice walked out of the front door, Samuel practically jumped from the buggy. He held her hand as she climbed up the footstep to the bench. It now seemed too narrow to Allan. That little bench did not allow any space between the two young people. Allan thought he might be starting to cold sweat.

Still, he knew there could be no better choice for his little girl. Samuel Menlach showed courtesy in the tiniest of gestures. He had been raised well by his parents and had the makings of a good man. Somewhere under a father's dread, Allan liked the boy and it made him happy that Alice found a good reason to stay.

As an afterthought, Samuel sheepishly asked, "Do you mind if Miss Howarth rides to church with me?"

"I wouldn't want her riding with anyone else," said Allan, choking back a small sob.

Almost as soon as Samuel urged his horse to go, Ben Abrim rode up in a similar carriage.

"I had a feeling you might need a ride. We should go, as I left my house in the care of Mrs. Menlach. She is a woman of immense patience, but she will not let me skirt my duties," said Ben Abrim.

The call of the morning birds told Allan that spring was near. They had been having unusually warm weather, but no one started their spring planting yet. The gentle bounce of the buggy seat rocked Allan peacefully.

He said, "I think my daughter is in love with the Menlach boy. Did you know about this?"

Ben Abrim grinned slightly. He said, "I see a lot of things. I am not surprised. Samuel Menlach is a good boy. If he has started courting your Alice, then Amos Menlach should count his blessings to be gaining a daughter."

Allan felt like he almost fell out of the buggy. He took the second breath-bating blow of the day. He said, "Wait a minute. Who said anything about marriage?"

"My apologies, Mr. Howarth," said Ben Abrim. "I will not spare your pride. We Amish do not casually intermingle like so many Englishers. If young Samuel is courting your Alice, then he has serious intentions. That does not mean they will be getting married next week. I will tell you the boy has not taken rumspringa yet. And by the word of Mrs. Menlach, he does plan to go up to Chicago. It would be at least a year before they are joined."

Allan pulled a handkerchief from his coat pocket and dabbed his forehead. He asked, "What am I supposed to do? I heard once that Amish paint the door of their house."

"Mein Gott, Englishers do have a talent for exaggeration. Your daughter is no fatted calf and you do not have to paint your door. This is a marriage, not a sacrifice. Courtship is a private thing. There is very little for you to do, papa."

When they arrived at Ben Abrim's house, the families of Karsten Field greeted Allan with many hugs and blessings. The men and boys ushered Allan into Ben Abrim's living room, which had been segregated with several rows of chairs on one side for men and on the other for women. Almost eighty people crowded into the modest building, but a cool breeze through the open windows kept everyone comfortable.

Ben Abrim stood in the middle of the room. He looked a little nervous, maybe shy, Allan thought.

"Friends, before we begin," said Ben Abrim, "I would like to welcome you into my home and thank God for this glorious day he has given us to gather and worship. This is the first time our new brother, Mr. Howarth, has joined us. We are also grateful to have his daughter with us."

Allan felt at home and appreciated Ben Abrim's kind words. He looked across the room at Alice and caught her staring at Samuel. Allan smiled at this and turned his attention back to Ben Abrim.

The older, always smiling, man continued, "I have one other announcement. Mr. Howarth has had quite an experience over the past few months. However, he has overcome tremendously, by God's hand, and taken to our ways without conscience. And if Mr. Howarth will forgive my intrusion, I would like to invite you all to his barn raising."

Some of the kids cheered and several adults applauded. Allan did not know what to say. He had not thought about what to do after he cleared the remains of the old barn. He smiled at his friend.

Ben Abrim continued, "He has worked diligently clearing away the wreckage without letting his duties at the school slip. We are all family and family helps one another. I propose that as soon as the ground is dry that we raise the Howarth barn."

From there, Ben Abrim turned the service over to Elder Tibold. The older man read from the bible with severity. Allan clearly saw that the man took his scripture very seriously. Beyond that, Allan did not get much of the day's message. His mind reveled in the open hearts of his new friends. He thought about his daughter growing from a little girl to a woman. For a brief moment, he imagined himself as a grandfather. He wished Tina would be here to share that with him, but then let that feeling pass. He missed his ex-wife, but he no longer felt the pain of it. He let that weight drop away, like so much of his former life.

Allan looked around the room at his new family. Almost all of them sat with bowed heads, reading along with Elder Tibold. Several of the children fidgeted, looking like tightly wound jack-in-the-boxes. Allan could feel all of the wonder and peace that awaited him. Then a pair of eyes caught his as he finished the sweep of the room. The teacher, Ms. Reece, instantly flicked her eyes back to her scripture.

It was decided, on such a fine day, that lunch would be served outdoors. Allan helped Luke Lenaxel's oldest boy John carry one of the tables. While most of the women finished setting out the food, Allan watched Ms. Reece entertaining the children. He saw a side of her that she did not display in the classroom. Her smile glistened and her eyes looked vibrant, surrounded by laughing children.

After lunch, little Ethel Kurtz led the children in the first of many songs. The entire congregation of Karsten Field spent the rest of the afternoon singing songs of praise. Allan did not know any of the words to any of the songs, but he felt uplifted. He wondered if church would be the same in two weeks at the Fencil house.

Samuel and Alice left before he did, but Allan made it home first. He waited on the front porch, listening to an orchestra of newborn crickets until the buggy appeared over the hill. As they came closer, Allan could hear the young couple quietly laughing. He decided to go into the house, so they could say a private good night. When Alice came inside, he hugged her without a word.

That night, Allan slept deeply and peacefully.

CHAPTER SIX

HE IS RISEN

Reflection

In the dark.

Alone.

Allan sat on the edge of his bed, staring at his hands, but not really seeing them.

Waiting for the sun to rise, he did not bother to light a candle. Instead, he traced the healing cuts and callouses on his hands with his sore fingertips. At this time of day, self-doubt kept him company.

He had no reason to doubt himself. For the first time, he felt like God had a hand in his life. He felt he had a purpose and he felt free. He broke free. He knew his old life was going to kill him. Probably literally. The stress and unhappiness could have easily given him a heart attack or stroke.

Allan pressed his hands together.

He did not miss that old life. Here in Karsten

Field, he had his health and new friends. He believed he was on a path to God that he would have otherwise missed.

He did not miss his old life.

He missed Tina.

How could he not miss the woman with which he spent nearly half of his life?

The bed creaked under his weight as Allan shifted. He did not know what time it was and wanted to go back to sleep. He should not be unhappy. He knew Tina would be better off without him. He hoped he would be fine without her.

These thoughts did not come to him often. He never really internalized her leaving, but he knew his wife deserved to have her own freedom. God would not have brought him here, if he was supposed to be unhappy. Allan tried to take his mind away from Tina.

Thoughts of Mary Reece replaced that.

Allan braced himself against those thoughts. He had only been separated from Tina for a couple months. He did not think it would be right to entertain thoughts of a new relationship. Still, the schoolteacher put those thoughts in his head with her out of place comments and stolen glances.

The morning birds interrupted Allan's contemplations. Their chirping outside his window told him that he would not be going back to sleep. Allan focused on the dim rectangle taking shape in his black field of vision. Soon the sun would be up high enough that his one window would light the entire bedroom. For now, it remained a dim rectangle.

Tina.

He wanted her to be happy. He knew she could move on from him.

Mary.

Not even a consideration. He only recently had truly become part of Karsten Field and did not want to upset anyone. He believed Elder Tibold, and probably a few others, would not approve.

A new sound interrupted his thoughts. The clinking of pans on the stove could only be Alice. She somehow managed to wake before him almost every day. She also somehow managed to make him breakfast before she headed off to the Menlachs'.

Allan knew what motivated her.

Samuel.

Almost since the first day they arrived in Karsten Field, she had been taken by the handsome young man. She used Mrs. Menlach as an excuse to go to their house any time she could.

The frequent visits served a greater purpose. Alice learned to cook and Allan enjoyed it very much. She seemed to have a natural ability in the kitchen that Tina never did. Sarah Menlach taught his daughter other skills that he could not imagine Alice doing. Allan suspected the Menlachs saw the budding romance long before he did. He also suspected Sarah Menlach of taking such a great interest in Alice only to ensure a suitable wife for her son.

The smell of breakfast crawled in under his wooden door. Coupled with the growing light at his window, Allan had no choice but to get out of bed.

By the light of the window, Allan looked at his hands again. He finished clearing the last of his ruined barn three weeks ago, but still had not managed to clean all of the black ash from under his fingernails. He did not mind much. It served as a reminder of his task. In a way, he considered it a penance for his old life.

Allan splashed some water on his face from the porcelain basin on his dresser. The cool water washed away his darker thoughts. It reminded him of his second baptism since coming to Karsten Field.

As Matthew Fencil said, Elder Tibold conducted baptisms on the day he held church at his house. Allan had the forethought to ask to be included. He already believed the baptism performed by Ben Abrim was enough. The emotions and circumstances of that event would always stay with him. He could still feel the cold of the January river, especially when he was alone on mornings like these.

Allan did his best to memorize and recite the Dordrecht. Boys, young men, half his age did far better. Still, Allan managed to get through it. He could feel Elder Tibold's compassion as the old man dunked him in the considerably warmer water. He felt the grip of a friend on his back and shoulder. To Allan, his first experience with Ben Abrim would be his baptism. The day in March marked the day that Elder Tibold stopped shunning Allan.

These thoughts moved Allan into a better state of mind. Being accepted by the whole of the congregation gave him a renewed sense of purpose and being. He had been looking forward to today and decided to get started.

After dressing quickly in his Saturday work clothes, Allan joined his daughter at their small table.

Alice set a warm plate of scrambled eggs in front of Allan along with what seemed like half a loaf of sourdough bread.

"I can't eat all this," Allan started to humbly protest.

"You need the extra carbs today," said Alice. "Besides, you better enjoy those eggs."

Allan looked at the plate of probably four eggs. He did not see any unusual or extra ingredients, only the yellow of scrambled yolk. "Why?" he asked.

"Because those are the last ones we are getting from the Menlachs," said Alice. "Starting tomorrow, we are going to have our own chickens in that barn you are building today. I think Samuel had a great idea to put the coop in there too."

His daughter's face beamed with an excited smile. Allan could tell in the smile that she wanted this life as much as he did. Every day, they became more a part of Karsten Field. It excited him to see her excited. The flash of her straight white teeth reminded him of the twelve-year-old girl she used to be. When she wore braces, she refused to smile at all. She went so far as to swear she would never smile again. Seeing Alice smile now made him glad that pre-teenage girls rarely keep such extreme promises.

Before Alice sat down, she put a small basket in the middle of the table. A hand painted egg rested in the basket. Allan studied the wavy red lines surrounded by yellow, with blue polka dots. It took Allan a moment to understand the meaning.

"For Easter," said Alice.

"Today?" Allan could not quite get his head around the date. Without his cellphone or his Google calendar, time took on a new meaning for him.

"No. Easter is tomorrow. The Easter Bunny doesn't come to Karsten Field, but Sarah painted a few eggs with Katie and Annie, so I made one for you," explained Alice.

She got up from the table and dashed into her bedroom. She returned before Allan could ask why she left. In her hands, she held a straw hat. Allan examined the perfectly round brim and the simple black band.

"I made this for you, too," Alice said. "It is going to be too hot to be wearing your felt hat. Now you have a summer hat."

Allan stood and hugged his daughter. It made him incredibly happy that she found a way to be part of his life. At the same time, a deep sadness stung his heart. He missed his son.

Construction

The sound of approaching horses caused Allan to break his embrace. He shoveled the last of his eggs into his mouth and tore off a hunk of bread. Allan placed his new hat on his head as he walked out the front door.

From his porch, Allan could make out Luke Lenaxel seated with his son John on their large work wagon. The sun had climbed to the top of the nearby line of trees and started to spill onto their work area. Luke volunteered to be the foreman. It had been more than a few years since their last barn raising, but Luke was foreman then, so it seemed appropriate.

"Thanks for coming," Allan called from his porch.

"It is a good thing we are doing," said Luke.

Allan followed Luke's wagon around the side of his house. He could see the thick beams in the back of the wagon that would make up the main supports of the barn. It still amazed Allan that everything they needed to build the barn was going to be donated. Luke had the four by six beams. Daniel Esch offered to bring the bulk of the lumber and nails. His family ran the furniture shop for the tourists. He said he had been blessed with an abundance of wood from the previous season and now had a good use for it.

By the time the sun displayed its full roundness above the trees, every male over the age of sixteen in Karsten Field had arrived. Luke set up a shaded area for Elder Tibold, Ben Abrim and Michael Miller, or as Allan privately thought of them, the gray-beards. Miller's oldest daughter married Tibold's son, Matthew, which made Tibold and Michael practically inseparable at any gathering.

Before Tibold took his supervisory seat, he came to Allan. He said, "You should know this is highly unusual, working the day before Easter."

"I appreciate..." started Allan.

Tibold continued as if Allan had not spoken at all, "As Mr. Zook continually reminds me, there is very little about you that is usual. As such, I expect you will lead a prayer before we begin work in earnest."

Allan could not decide if Tibold was asking him to lead the prayer or if it was a statement. Regardless, Allan said, "I would be glad to."

After they laid out the tools and tended to the horses, all twenty-nine fathers and sons gathered in a circle on the ground that had once been and soon would be a barn. They locked hands and lowered their heads.

Allan started by thanking his friends. "I am blessed to have such brothers," he said. "We begin this day in the eyes of our Lord to work for his glory. As You raised up Your only son, so we raise up this barn that it may yield nourishment for Your children. The glory of this day is Yours and any good that we do is because of and for You.

Easter is a time of renewal, so from this ash covered ground, we begin again." He decided to end with a quote from the Dordrecht, "May you Lord, through Your grace, make us all worthy and meet, that this may befall none of us; but that we may thus take heed unto ourselves, and use all diligence, that on that day we may be found before You unspotted and blameless in peace. Amen."

Hearty shouts of "Amen" echoed his own. Allan could see that these men were ready to work.

They set to work with a soundtrack provided by the last of the morning birds. Chirping interspersed the sounds of construction. The serrated teeth of the handsaw created its own music as several of the men cut away at the heavy beams.

Luke Lenaxel reminded them, "Measure twice. Cut once."

Allan had been assigned to digging postholes. Two-man teams took up positions at the four corners of the planned barn. Allan worked with Samuel Menlach. He suspected his daughter's "boyfriend" purposely joined him at this hole. The youth must have felt an obligation to prove himself. What Samuel did not know was that Allan already considered him worthy simply because Alice did. If this young man was cause enough for his daughter to change her life, then that was all the reason Allan needed.

The two men dug the hole in silence and in less than ten minutes, they were the first to have their hole ready. Mr. Lenaxel guided a team carrying the first post to Allan's hole. Using a plumb swinging at the center of a tripod, Luke Lenaxel watched them level the beam so it stood as near to perpendicular from the smooth ground as possible. Allan had grated the ground with a shovel and rake for hours to make it as smooth and level as possible. Now, he found his work to be more than satisfactory, as the men easily set the post in its upright position.

Almost as quickly, they erected the other three posts. They wasted no time in tying the corners together. Before they pulled the tall ladders from one of the wagons, the older Troyer boy boosted his brother onto his shoulders. Samuel followed suit by hefting John Lenaxel onto his. In this fashion, the four of them secured the corner posts, while the others began framing in the long sidewalls.

Both the front and back of the barn were going to have wide doors, according to Luke Lenaxel's plan. He wanted to wait on those until they at least had the rafters in place overhead. Allan could see the barn begin to take shape as they put the studs in place.

Above the main barn floor, some of the men started to hang joists that would make a smaller, second story for the barn. It looked to Allan like he would have about a ten-foot walkway along both sides and across the back of the second floor. Before they started on the walkway, they assembled the second story walls and hoisted them up into position. Ten men on the ground and ten balanced on homemade wooden ladders. With one hand steadying nails and the other swinging a hammer, Allan wondered how they held onto those ladders.

While this was Allan's barn, he felt like a puppet. He had no real experience in construction and no idea what the finished barn would look like, other than seeing his neighbors' barns. He did his best to follow instructions. The thing that impressed him most is that they did all of the work without a nail gun or drill or power saw. Getting used to living without electricity had been easier than Allan expected. However, this seemed to be one of those times that it would be acceptable to use power tools.

Resurrection

During a water break, Ben Abrim explained, "Idle hands are the Devil's playthings. We do our best to keep Lucifer from our doorstep. All great things have simple beginnings, so we keep it simple."

Mr. Lenaxel asked Allan to join them hanging the roof rafters. Allan climbed the wobbling ladder past the partially completed second floor. He glanced down for a moment and discovered he was uncomfortable at this height. He could only have been about twenty feet from the ground, but it might as well have been one hundred. Thoughts of broken bones danced in his head.

Allan moved off of the ladder and across the narrow lines of wood. From above, the barn resembled a jumbled criss-cross that could have been made from popsicle sticks. The men walking over the wide gaps and hanging from the sides made Allan think of spiders spinning a uniquely geometric web.

Shortness of breath made Allan realize how much he did not like heights. He did his best to keep his center of gravity low and managed to find a spot where he would not be in anybody else's way. One of the Troyer boys slid him a board and he began nailing it in place. Then a familiar voice caught his attention.

"Dad. Hey dad." The shout came from a distance, but it was unmistakable. Allan spun around to look for his son. He had to be on the ground somewhere, probably in front of the house, Allan guessed.

He started to call back, "Brett? Whoa!"

The sudden movement caused Allan to lose his balance. In an instant, the trees appeared to be growing from the sky. Then the world moved slower than it ever had before, at least from Allan's perspective. The mesh of boards sliced up the horizon into uniform puzzle pieces. Through some of the squares, he could make out faces. Each one belonged to a different man, but each had the same expression. Samuel Menlach, eyes wide. John Lenaxel, mouth agape. Isaac Gundy seemed to be yelling, but it did not reach Allan's ears.

The world stopped.

A hammer hung in mid-air. Allan's small tin of nails dotted the sky like sinister metallic rain drops. Then the ground replaced the sky. With each twist, the ground came closer. In the infinite time that Allan dropped from the roof of his barn, he had countless thoughts, including the end of his life.

One thought that stood out took him back to his youth. When he was seven years old, a friend dared him to jump off the high dive at the public pool. From the wet concrete, the three-meter board did not seem so high, but from the edge of the overly springy fiberglass board, it seemed incredibly high. Allan decided not to take the plunge, but before he could get down, his goading friend came up the ladder. Lifeguard whistles blurted their shrill sound. The warnings did not stop his friend from pushing Allan off the board to the waiting water. There is a moment after hitting the water between when inertia stops taking you down and buoyancy brings you to the surface, where Allan felt trapped. Helpless.

He felt that same suspended moment now.

He had to be getting closer to the ground. He knew things had to be happening faster that what they seemed.

Halfway between the roof and the ground, Allan heard another familiar voice. Only, he knew no one else could hear it. He had heard this voice several times since coming to Karsten Field. He wanted to believe it was the voice of God, or maybe Isaac Karsten from Ben Abrim's story.

The voice said, "I will lift you up."

Those five words took away Allan's fear. He no longer feared falling or getting hurt. Then he realized he was no longer falling. He gathered his wits and saw that he was hanging in mid-air. Nothing moved in slow motion. He saw several men coming toward him, crossing the rafters like skilled carpenters. He could hear other men cheering. Allan could feel a wide plank of wood under his back. He thought for a moment that an angel scooped him up, but now he realized he fell only a few feet onto a wide board that was not there a moment before he fell.

At the far end of his saving board, Allan could see Daniel Esch dangling from a ladder, mopping his brow with a sawdust-covered handkerchief. Apparently, Mr. Esch moved the board under Allan to save him from what could have been a fatal fall.

Safely on the ground, Brett rushed up to his father and hugged him fiercely. He forced out the words, "I'm sorry," while trying to hold back sobs.

"What are you sorry for?" asked Allan. He could not believe Brett was actually here.

"It's my fault," explained Brett. "I shouldn't have called to you. I made you fall."

Allan put his hands on his son's shoulders and held him at arm's length to look in his face. He said, "It's not your fault. I shouldn't have been up there in the first place. Maybe if you hadn't called to me right then, something worse might have happened?"

Daniel Esch seemed to have caught his breath

and joined the reunion. He explained to Allan that he was carrying the wide board up for the eaves at the back of the barn. The second he noticed Allan falling, something told him to shove the board between his ladder and the crossbeam on the side of the roof. Had he not been there, Allan understood, he would have fallen all the way to the hard-packed dirt.

"Praise God for guiding my hand," said Daniel. "I had intended to carry the board around the long way and carry it up a ladder back there. At the last moment, I chose to go up first and then across the roof to the back. You were saved by God's grace alone."

Allan wanted to ask Mr. Esch if he heard any voices leading him to his decision. He decided not to stir that particular pot. The voices and laughter of women and children ended their conversation. The wives and daughters of Karsten Field had arrived with lunch.

Ham sandwiches and fresh spring vegetable soup filled hungry bellies. Allan sat with Brett and Alice.

"Did your mother come with you?" asked Allan.

"No, but she bought my bus ticket. I don't have to go back until Monday," said Brett.

"Are you off school for Easter?"

"Come on, dad. I go to a public school. They call it a *teacher work day*," said Brett.

They finished their ample lunch while Brett updated them on his return to school and how Tina was dealing with her mother. Apparently, her illness had gotten worse which kept Tina home more. Allan imagined how much worse it would have been for Tina if she had been here instead of with her mother.

When they finished eating, Brett asked, "Can I help?"

"Do you know which end of the hammer to hold?" asked Allan.

"Probably about as good as you," said Brett.

They both stopped at this. Then they exploded with laughter. They started laughing so uncontrollably that everyone gathered around the skeleton of a barn stopped to look at them. Ben Abrim mingled nearby and leaned in to share in the joke. Allan explained that Brett offered to help.

Ben Abrim smiled his famous smile. He said, "Seeing as we would not be gathered here today if not for the boy, I see no reason why he should not help. Go to Mr. Lenaxel there. He will give you a job."

Brett hurried off and Allan started to follow. Ben Abrim gently took Allan by the elbow to stop him.

He said, "It is good to see you with your son. Has he decided to stay with you?"

"I don't think so," said Allan. "He is only here for the weekend." Allan started to walk away, then added, "You know, I'm okay with that. A part of me wishes I had my whole family with me, but we were not a family for a long time before that. I think we all need some room to grow. Our roots were getting tangled."

"Ah, but your roots will grow down into God's love and keep you strong," said Ben Abrim. "He's a smart boy and I know he will make the right decisions. They may not lead him back here, but they will help him walk in God's light."

The rest of the day seemed more like a party than hard labor. Children ran around, playing tag and hide-and-seek. The women made sure they had plenty of whoopie pies and lemonade. Allan made sure to stay on the ground, but he and Brett did their share of the work. What looked like an out-of-control erector set a few short hours ago now resembled a solid piece of craftsmanship. As the sun started to set, John Lenaxel pounded away at shingles on the roof with Max and Reimy, the Troyer boys. Luke Lenaxel oversaw the hinges on the front and back doors.

Elder Tibold and Mr. Miller headed home, as did most of the fathers, especially the ones with younger children.

Ben Abrim remained to inspect the finished product with Allan.

"Mr. Howarth, I believe you have a barn," said Ben Abrim.

"I believe you are right, Mr. Zook," said Allan. "Brett headed over to the Menlachs' to pick out some chickens."

"Don't forget, I have your two cows in my barn."

"Ha." Allan laughed out loud. "I don't know the first thing about cows. Between working on the barn and chores at the school, I haven't been near an animal except the kittens Ethel Kurtz brought to class."

"I wouldn't worry about that. I think you will have a good teacher in young Sam Menlach," Ben Abrim gestured to the young man standing by Allan's front porch. Samuel held a hammer, but he was not using it. It appeared that he and Alice were in the middle of an important conversation. The way she leaned over the rail reminded him of that scene from Romeo and Juliet. From inside his barn, across the yard and lit only by a few lanterns, Allan could see a spark in his daughter's eyes. Samuel seemed to be working hard, but he was done with the barn.

"I suspect Samuel will be more than willing to come around to help with the animals," continued Ben Abrim.

Allan surveyed the barn one last time before they extinguished the last of the lanterns. A simple, rectangular building with a three-sided balcony. Luke tested the wide doors before he locked them with a sliding wood latch. Allan figured the new barn had more square footage than the one Brett burned to the ground.

Ben Abrim started to say his good nights. "Tomorrow we will be fasting and I trust you will recite scripture with your children."

"No Easter egg hunt?" joked Allan.

"Oh, yes, the Easter Rabbit is not a part of our celebration," said Ben Abrim. "When God in Heaven resurrected His only son, He did not leave a basket of colored eggs and candy in the tomb. No, it is a time for reflection and prayer. However, on Easter Monday, I expect you will join us at Mr. Gundy's for a family meal. It is his year to host and as you know he has a blessed hand when it comes to smoked meats."

Dissolution

After helping Mr. Lenaxel pack up the last of his tools, Allan joined Alice and Samuel on the front porch to wait for Brett. David Menlach delivered Brett and two chickens in exchange for picking up his younger brother. Allan and his children settled the chickens into their new coop.

"David said the black one should have eggs in the morning, but the brown one is stubborn," offered Brett.

Once inside the house, Brett started to unpack his bag. Underneath a couple plain white tees, he pulled out a manila envelope.

"Mom asked me to give this to you," he said, handing the envelope to Allan.

Allan looked at the very legal sounding collection of names in the upper left corner of the envelope and knew exactly what he would find inside. As if looking might somehow change the outcome, Allan slid out the surprisingly thin stack of papers. Across the top of the first page, he read "Petition for Divorce". Allan pushed the papers back into the envelope and put the whole thing face down on the corner of the table.

He knew he would not sleep, despite being exhausted and having a near death experience.

He could not rest with that packet of papers whispering to him. After Brett and Alice went to sleep, Allan lit a small candle and put it on their table. He took the papers out and flipped through them, not really reading.

His mind skipped around his memories. He thought about his wedding day. He remembered being in the room for the birth of both of his children. He remembered the time their basement flooded from an unexplainable broken water line. It seemed like so long ago, but he did have good memories of being married to Tina. Allan corrected himself, great memories. But that was in the past. They grew apart, that is the excuse that broken couples used. Allan knew he had a purpose in his new life. It made him sad that it would not include Tina, but she was not part of God's plan for him.

Allan stared at the one blank line requesting his signature. One line to erase decades of their life. Allan thought about how simply the legality of marriage could destroy the sanctity of marriage. Underneath all of it, he knew Tina would be fine. He knew he would be fine.

Allan picked up his pen and set Tina free.

CHAPTER SEVEN

LOVE IN BLOOM

Routine

Visits with Brett became a regular thing. Allan began to develop a strong relationship with his son.

Brett came at least one weekend a month, sometimes every other weekend. For those two days, the father and son did everything together. Brett did not shy away from any chores. On Sundays that they did not have church, they started learning to fish.

Allan and Brett met Ben Abrim and several other fathers and sons down by the river. They intended for the activity to be a relaxing break from their other labors. However, teaching Allan how to thread a hook and cast a line became as much of a chore as milking a stubborn cow. Brett had an easier time with it. Allan attributed that to his son's hand-eye coordination, honed from years of video games.

None of the men spoke much while fishing, except to give thanks when someone pulled out a large catfish, or the occasional walleye caught out after its bedtime. Mostly, they spent the time communing with the Lord, reflecting on the past week and planning for the next.

Allan imagined it to be quite a site. Ten, fifteen and sometimes up to twenty men and boys silently lined up on the bank, the random whirs of line unspooling, plops of hooks and anchors hitting the water.

Aside from milk and eggs, Allan's meals came either from his trips to the river or from his neighbors. Karsten Field took care of its own. Allan felt a little guilty, but at the same time, Ben Abrim shared the same situation, as did the schoolteacher, Mary Reece. In a way, he felt as if he was taking advantage, but he also did not have the years of knowledge or the extra hands. The fact that Alice helped Sarah Menlach everyday made him feel a little better about sharing their food.

Brett seemed to enjoy his visits too. He got up early to work in the barn and stayed up late talking to his father.

"I like this," he said, one Saturday night.

"Me too," started Allan. Not sure exactly what Brett meant, he added, "Like what?"

"Getting away. I mean, I couldn't do it all the time. Not like you," said Brett. "But it's good to unplug. At least for a few days, I don't have to sort through a wall of pointless Facebook updates or tweet about who's dating who."

"I didn't date anyone until I was sixteen," said Allan. "Of course, we didn't have Facebook then either. We actually had to talk to people, in person."

They both laughed at this. While Brett faded into a chuckle, Allan stopped short. His momentary joy transformed into something more profound. At this moment, he shared a connection with his son. He caught a glimpse of the man the boy would become and he liked what he saw. Allan considered it a blessing to have that foresight. As Ben Abrim had said, Allan believed Brett would grow in God's light.

Allan loved his new relationship with his son. Maybe they only saw each other a few days a month, but they shared more than when they lived together. Before Karsten Field, Allan would come home from work to what seemed like an empty house. When his kids were home, they stayed up in their bedrooms. Unless they shared a family meal, Allan literally went days without seeing Brett or Alice, in his old life.

Now, Allan had mature, insightful conversations with Brett. It made him feel even better that Brett did not bring bad news with him on every visit. After returning the papers that Brett gave him the weekend of the barn raising, the boy had nothing but good news. Brett said that Tina found a good new job with a schedule that allowed her to take care of her mother and make sure the ailing woman made it to doctor's appointments and such.

It seemed that Allan's ex-wife started to have

her own life and it seemed to be going good. Besides having a better relationship with his father, it appeared that Brett's relationship with his mother grew as well. Brett talked about the new things they did together and how he took on many responsibilities around the house. It made Allan feel good that Tina could move on without him.

Eighteen

Allan also started to have meaningful conversations with Alice. He secretly always felt a little closer to her. He suspected that had to do with her being the first-born and being named after him. Many people did not get the reference, but when he explained his name was Allan Joseph and hers was Alice Josephine, people would say, "Oh, I get it." He wondered sometimes if they did, but it really did not matter. She was his baby girl and always would be.

The problem with Alice's talks is that they all centered on one thing.

Samuel.

Allan knew Sam Menlach was a fine young man. He showed courtesy and respect to everyone. He made it a point to ask Allan's permission each time he took Alice to church or any other gathering. They spent most of every day together, but neither of them let it interfere with their duties.

This did not seem like the daughter Allan used to know. Before coming here, Alice seemed to never think of anyone but herself. Every father believes his daughter is beautiful, but Allan could never believe how Alice's beauty came from his DNA.

Even at sixteen, she was repeatedly approached to do modeling. She had a string of what Allan considered "loser" boyfriends. The one good thing that Allan learned second-hand from Tina was that Alice chose never to "be with" any of those boys. He could never have the nerve to say it to her, but Allan respected his daughter for having the control and self-esteem to "save" herself. Apparently, in that private mother-daughter conversation, Alice definitively said she would wait until she was married.

"I'm not dumb, mom," Alice once said. "I know I don't have to share my body to make somebody like me. If he doesn't like me for me, then that's his problem."

Despite Alice's rebellious teenage years, Allan knew he and Tina had done at least one good thing together. They raised independent children with an extra helping of self-respect.

Thinking back on those recent years, Allan almost did not recognize his daughter now. Her dark hair, usually with a red or purple streak, now stayed tucked neatly under her kapp. Her ninety-minute bathroom and makeup rituals had been reduced to a soap and water scrub. The lack of blushes and rouges made Alice shine even more in Allan's eyes. Without the trappings and demands of the outside world, Alice discovered how to show her true, natural beauty.

She even adapted to the seemingly strict, but acceptable clothing requirements. Alice had never been afraid to show her slender, toned body. She competed in high school athletics and even bought herself a summer gym membership. Warm weather usually meant fewer clothes. She seemed to easily accept the new requirements almost from the first day. Allan did not know if Sarah Menlach explained it to his daughter. He, however, knew what temptations could come from Alice's short shorts and spaghetti strap tops. Thankfully, Alice had a way of making whatever she wore into her own. The long dresses suited her as well as short skirts. Best of all to Allan, she did not complain about it.

He assumed for all of those changes he had to thank Samuel Menlach. So when the conversation unavoidably fell to "Samuel this" or "Samuel that", Allan absorbed it with a grin.

Samuel also played another great role in Allan's life. Being the second oldest son of Amos Menlach, he did not share the same responsibilities as his older brother, David. David had an eye for Mr. Kinzinger's oldest daughter, June, but even more of an eye for his own father's farm. David felt it a duty to take over for Amos, like Kinzinger's oldest boy would take over their farm. The question was *if*, not *when*, he would decide to marry June.

"He may marry this dirt before a good woman," Amos told Allan one day. "David is a good boy and he honors his father by working so hard."

David's earnest attitude and reliability freed Samuel to spend time with Allan and Alice. Samuel showed Allan what chores needed to be done in the barn. He smiled at work like cleaning the chicken coop, an act that caused Allan to gag more than once. The thought of eating an egg so close to its point of origin almost put Allan off them altogether.

Sam also helped repair the old split rail fences behind the barn, so the cows could graze. He insisted that the natural grasses would yield better milk than grain from a trough.

Shortly after they finished Allan's new barn, Samuel and Ben Abrim took Allan into the field behind his house.

"You have maybe five acres here," said Samuel. "It is not much."

Allan looked at the field. It seemed big to him, far larger than any yard in his old neighborhood. It definitely looked bigger than something he would want to mow, even on a riding mower.

"It is the size that is needed. It is enough for you and your child to stay fed and give back to the others," said Ben Abrim.

Give back? Allan did want to return the kindness that had been shown to him. He did not always want to feel like he was eating everyone else's food or taking their clothing. He was not quite sure what Ben Abrim and Samuel had in mind, but he could not say *no*.

"What do I have to do?" asked Allan.

Samuel's smile grew wider than usual. He said, "We are going to work this land. I will help you get started and show you what needs to be done. In no time, you will handle this by yourself."

"You want me to farm?" said Allan, feeling stunned. "I don't know anything about growing crops. I've been lucky so far mending fences and patching roofs."

Ben Abrim said, "Leave the growing of the grain to our Father. You can use my horse to pull the plow. If you can work the soil, God will provide the rain and sun. Come this fall, you will be surprised what you can or cannot do. Your small patch of land will add nicely to our winter stores."

Allan looked across the field again. Both Ben Abrim and Samuel called it small, but the five acres seemed huge to Allan. He almost let himself feel defeated by the coming task. Then it occurred to him that he could do it. With everything else he had been through, plowing a field would be one of the easier things. Maybe God was testing his strength, so Allan intended to show his worth.

With that, working his field became a part of the routine. Allan started his day at five in the morning. He let the cows out to graze, while he worked the field. Clearing the weeds and small trees that had taken root took a couple weeks. Then Samuel showed him how to turn the earth and prepare it for planting. The ground had not been planted in many years, so it took more than a couple passes to get down to the dark, rich, fertile soil.

After working the field, Allan brushed Ben Abrim's horse. He then brought the cows back to the barn for milking. He felt like a soldier on the front line raiding the chicken coop. The chickens made a lot of noise, but Allan always managed to come away with enough eggs for the next morning's breakfast.

Convene

If things went well, Allan could get cleaned up and make it to the school by ten o'clock. There he would do any chores that needed doing or read scripture while he waited for Ms. Reece to break for lunch. After lunch, Allan helped the kids practice their arithmetic. It felt natural for his aching hands to be covered in chalk dust. Writing on the green slate reminded him of being a kid in elementary school. He knew Brett did most of his schoolwork on an iPad and the chalkboards had been replaced with white boards and smart boards.

Allan once calculated interest rates and mortgage payments. Working hard on his field and spending so much time alone with his thoughts, he felt relief in the rote two plus two's.

"Why?" asked little Ethel Kurtz one day. Allan had known her to be a wonderful singer and good friend, even to the older kids. Her question surprised him coming from someone so young.

She asked again, "Why does two plus two equal four?"

"Because it does," stated Allan.

"But why?" she asked again.

Ms. Reece stood up from her desk, "Ethel Kurtz, do we need to go out behind the schoolhouse? It is not your place to tease adults."

"But I'm not teasing, Ms. Reece. Please don't make me get a switch," begged little Ethel.

Allan appreciated Ms. Reece's sense of discipline, but he did not think Ethel was making a joke. He knew the children of Karsten Field to be well mannered and well behaved. They had loving families and an excellent teacher. It would not be like any of them to make fun at another's expense. While little Ethel Kurtz could be precocious, he believed her question to be sincere.

"Ah, you know, that is a good question," said Allan. He hoped his response would belay any scolding from Ms. Reece. He had never seen her use a switch on any of the students, but the threat was there for that rare instance. Allan continued, "How many fingers am I holding up?"

He pointed his index finger of his right hand to the sky and closed the rest of his fingers into a fist.

"One," said Ethel.

"Now, how many is it in German?" he asked, not changing his hand.

"Eine," volunteered one of the boys, before Ethel could answer.

"Did you know in Spanish, it is *uno*?" asked Allan.

Several of the students repeated "uno".

"But we do not speak Spanish, Mr. Howarth," interjected Mary Reece.

"Exactly," said Allan. "But no matter what language we speak, and God's children speak a lot of different languages, this value never changes." Allan waved his index finger around the whole classroom. "From here to Pennsylvania, one is one."

Then Allan held up a second finger. On his left hand, he held up two more fingers. He said, "It really doesn't matter what we call them, but two plus two is always four. God gave us these wonderful fingers to grab things with, but they are also perfect for counting." Then he wiggled all of his fingers at the class.

The students giggled and began counting their own fingers, wiggling at each other and giggling some more. Allan did not think he really answered little Ethel's question, but she seemed satisfied along with the rest of the students. Ms. Reece even gave Allan a veiled, but approving smile.

Unforeseen

One Sunday, after Brett headed for the bus stop, Alice and Samuel asked to have a private conversation with Allan. It made him a little nervous trying to guess what they might want to talk about in private.

They sat at the small table in their main room. A candle flicked bravely at the coming sunset outside the front window. Samuel seemed somewhat anxious himself, but, as Allan expected, Alice took the lead. He always admired her for being unafraid to speak her mind, even against his own fatherly directives.

"Dad, you know Sam and I have gotten close?" she said.

Allan braced himself for what was coming next. He knew Tina always thought he was the typical clueless male, but he had become more in tune with his world. His relationship with his daughter had clarified and solidified. He suspected this talk would be about marriage.

"I...I know," he said.

Alice continued, "Well, Sam hasn't taken his rumspringa yet. He's knows it will leave you alone with the farm, but he wants to go this summer so he can be baptized next spring."

A tenseness Allan had not felt released from his body. He pictured himself wiping his forehead, saying "whew" like in a comic strip.

He said, "Is that all? You're worried about me? Please, Samuel, I know rumspringa is pretty important. Don't worry about me. I'll be fine, but I can say you won't find anything like Karsten Field in the outside world."

Samuel's cheeks flushed red. He said, "Mr. Howarth, I appreciate that. I already have my father's permission. He says that you have unusual character and that you will do well on your own. All the same, I felt obliged to ask your permission. Also, I agree. I know I will return to Karsten Field. This is my one chance to see the world about which Alice has told me so much. I know I won't find anything better out there, especially not her."

Allan appreciated Samuel's comments and compliments, but before he could say anything, Alice interrupted him.

"He wants me to go with him! We want to go to Chicago," she said.

This statement hit Allan almost as hard as a marriage proposal would have. He was not prepared for either.

"You what?" he stammered.

"I've always wanted to go to Chicago," said Alice. "It would be so much better than Des Moines. We talked about staying with Mom, but then decided it would be better to be on our own. We could see museums, baseball games, Fourth of July. Samuel's never seen fireworks. We would not even be gone a whole year. We would be back in time for baptism and then we can get married right after that."

Alice delivered so much information in one breath that Allan almost could not process it all. One word crashed into his brain. She tagged it on to the end of an eloquent speech, but Allan locked onto the m-word. He had only recently gotten his daughter back. He thought their relationship was going so well. Now she wanted to leave him. Not for a few months or a year, but for the rest of their lives.

He knew she was not abandoning him. He believed they firmly intended to return to Karsten Field. But marriage changed the relationship between a parent and child. His whole life had been about taking care of her and suddenly she would be taking care of someone else. He could not ask for a better son-in-law, but he was not ready to let go of his baby girl. Sitting on the chair across from him, he could only picture a three-year-old girl, squirming on his knee, looking up at him like he was her whole world. How did she become this incredible woman, he wondered.

"What do you think?" Alice's voice broke him from his thoughts.

"What do I think?" Allan repeated. What did he think? He searched his heart and called out to that voice in his head. He needed words from a power greater than himself. The only thing that echoed in his head was *set free*. Those words did not come from some mysterious voice. This time, they came from his own heart. Whatever outside force guided him here, it was now a part of his life. He shook off the selfish urges and needs. He dropped the worries of being alone. What did he think? He did not think anything. He felt it and it felt good.

Finally, Allan said, "I think it is fantastic."

Samuel's entire body seemed to sag with the same relief that Allan now felt. Alice laughed and cried at the same time.

"I've been watching you two," said Allan.

"God has matched you up perfectly. You go to Chicago and I will be waiting for you right here when you get back."

Alice got up from her chair and squeezed her father tightly. The only thing Allan could think was that those precious arms did not use to go all the way around his body.

The days passed too quickly for Allan and he found himself waving goodbye to his daughter and future son-in-law. They boarded the bus for Chicago with looks of wonder and anticipation. The whole Menlach family joined him and Ben Abrim to bid them a safe journey. Sarah Menlach cried enough for all of them, which got both sets of her twins in tears.

For the first time since moving to Karsten Field, Allan slept alone in an empty house. He declined Ben Abrim's offer of using the old man's spare bed. Allan had no one to talk to in the dark, but he did not feel lonely. His skin burned warm from the stirring emotions underneath. He had never felt more loved, more a part of something. He fell asleep and dreamed of tucking his small children in bed.

Intervene

Whispered talk of rumspringa danced around the classroom over the next week. The older boys and girls marveled the younger children with stories of world travel and fanciful adventures. Allan tried to see the world through their innocent eyes. It must seem like such a big place, especially without internet or cell phones to prematurely shorten the distance.

One particular day, the spring rains gave way to an unusually warm day. The students had almost eight weeks before Ms. Reece dismissed them for a month of summer break. They did their best not to complain, but Allan could tell the heat was getting to them.

"Ms. Reece, do you mind if I leave the front door open? I will be going in and out a lot stacking the left over firewood," said Allan.

She agreed. The kids looked relieved by the slight breeze and that made Allan happy. He really did not have that much wood to move, but purposely took his time as to allow them as much fresh air as possible.

For Allan, summer in the city meant heat, trips to the public pool and ice cream at the mall. He never gave a thought to what summer meant to the wild animals with which they shared their hills and fields.

Allan carried two logs out the door and around to the woodpile. His activity stirred an unseen creature that had been cooling itself in the shade of the previously undisturbed wood. Maybe out of instinct, or for some other reason, the creature gradually followed Allan back to the open door of the school.

Its three-foot long, twisting body moved silently on the dirt path. It made no sound and no other animal came along to scare it from its destination. It kept its copper-colored head low to the ground. A small, forked tongue darted out frequently sensing Allan's body heat and sweaty odor.

Allan had no idea that he was being followed by the venomous snake. If he could have felt what was in the snake's head, he would have felt confusion and curiosity. This creature would not normally hunt prey larger than itself, nor would it be attracted to the tumultuous noise of busy children. Unlike Allan, this copperhead snake would much rather be alone.

Inside the door, the snake curved against the wall and slid behind the row of student's lunch baskets. Allan walked straight ahead toward his office. Ms. Reece kept a pitcher of lemonade on a table in the back hall. As he chugged the cool liquid, he wondered why Ms. Reece made the lemonade every day. She never shared it with the students or drank it herself. That left Allan with the assumption that she made it only for him. He rather liked that idea.

Horrendous screams shattered Allan's pleasant beverage break. He dashed back into the classroom to find some desks toppled and students standing on others. The center of the room had been cleared as if a bomb exploded blowing everything outward in a circular pattern. At ground zero, Allan saw what caused the heart-racing commotion.

The hourglass pattern shifted on the snake's rusty brown back. The creature had to be as frightened as the children fleeing from it. It curled tight and raised its head, fangs exposed.

The next moment seemed like a dream when Allan tried to recall it. He did not have a clear recollection of the thought process. He joked later that Isaac Karsten guided his hand, but he had no better explanation.

Allan took two large steps across the room. In one fluid motion, he grabbed the poisonous snake's barely exposed tail. He snapped his arm away from his body. Keeping his eyes on the nearby children, he flung the copperhead out the open door without checking his aim. Then Allan moved as fast as he could to close the door. He watched the snake writhing on the ground for a moment. Out of nowhere, a horned owl swooped down and snatched the serpent. As suddenly as it appeared, the owl vanished into the woods with its meal.

Everyone decided to keep the door closed for the rest of the class day. The kids bubbled with excitement and fading terror. Ms. Reece decided they would accomplish very little and dismissed the class.

"I suggest that you share this experience with your family. Both the copperhead snake and horned owl are rarely seen. We should count our blessings to meet two of God's amazing animals in the same day," said Ms. Reece. "Be sure to tell your parents that you love them."

Allan noticed she did not explain the reason for giving love to their parents. She realized as much as he did that a bite from a copperhead could kill anyone of them before they could get help. He did assist in checking each student for any signs of a bite. Thankfully, no one was bitten.

After the kids left, Allan helped Ms. Reece straighten the classroom. They checked under every desk and in every corner to make certain no other friends had snuck into the schoolhouse. Then Allan prepared to head home. He usually did not stay up much past eight these days and still had to make dinner and a few other chores.

Mary Reece blocked his path.

"Good afternoon, Ms. Reece," he said.

"Mr. Howarth," she began. "What you did today. I thank God that you were here. I have a deep fear of snakes and fear something awful would have happened without you."

"It was nothing," said Allan, trying to hide his own shivers. He did not care for snakes either.

"Nothing? You grabbed a deadly animal with your bare hands. I would hardly call that nothing," said Ms. Reece.

Allan said, "I couldn't let it hurt any of the kids, or..." He paused, feeling an unfamiliar lump in his throat. "Or you."

"I have to say, Mr. Howarth, I do feel somewhat uncomfortable staying here alone tonight. If you would be kind enough to check the other rooms of the house, I could make dinner for us. Maybe by then my nerves will have calmed some."

Allan wanted to shout yes, like a teenage boy asking out a girl for a first date. It had only been a few months since Tina left, but their relationship had ended a few years before that. Allan never expected to start a new relationship so soon.

He had to reel himself in, had to correct his thinking. Mary Reece was not asking him for a date or a romantic evening. She offered to cook him a meal in exchange for ridding her house of a pest, albeit a venomous pest.

"Alright," he answered. "On one condition. I would like you to call me Allan."

Ms. Reece looked shocked. She must not have expected such familiarity and forwardness from him. Her expression slipped momentarily to a smile and then to her normally stoic face.

"Very well, Allan. Please do not expect this to be a regular occasion," she said. "Dinner will be ready at six, which gives you plenty of time to finish stacking the wood, check for snakes and wash yourself. And," she hesitated, "you may call me Mary when we are alone."

Allan finished his work and while he washed, he could not keep from smiling. A broad grin stretched across his cheeks. He felt something, but could not quite decide what. To think that it might be love gave him pause and a little guilt. He settled on infatuation. Mary Reece represented something new a different.

Allan wanted to discover what that meant.

Chapter Eight

The Loophole

Rendezvous

"Please do not expect this to be a regular occasion," Mary Reece told Allan almost ten weeks ago. Since that time, their evening meals together increased from once a week to five times in the past five days. Aside from dinners, they also started having Saturday lunch together. Once the children began their summer break from school, Ms. Reece started helping Allan with chores at his place. He, of course, continued to do double duty and keep up his work at the schoolhouse.

The best part of all of it for Allan was that Mary Reece continued to smile when they were together. He had come to know her as somewhat stern and often stoic. In these ten weeks, she gradually dropped that façade when they were alone. She seemed to take comfort in his company. Allan definitely enjoyed being with her.

Their conversations became less about school and more personal. She had yet to consent to riding to church with Allan. However, they got to know each other better than their formal interactions in front of the children at school.

One morning, Allan found Mary, crying in the barn. She must have dragged the milking stool into the chicken coop because she sat, partially hidden, in the corner, looking at the chickens. The birds clucked and pecked at the freshly strewn grain.

Mary sobbed, apparently nearing the end of her tears. She said, "This is difficult for me."

Allan pushed open the wire-covered door and stepped inside the coop. He said, "What is it, Mary?"

"I miss him," she said.

Mary did not say who she missed, but Allan could surmise. Ben Abrim had spoken briefly of Mary's deceased husband. Allan knew nothing about him. He did not know for certain how long he had been gone.

"You remind me of him," she continued. "Partly because of that, I think I have feelings for you."

Allan knelt in front of Mary. He wanted to comfort her. It took some effort, but he said, "I have feelings for you too."

"Does that not make you feel guilt?" A perplexed look crossed her face. "When I think of my husband, I feel unfaithful having thoughts of you. I know my God would not have led me to you if we were not meant to be together."

The thought of God bringing them together gave Allan pause. He did not come to Karsten Field looking for a new relationship. He thought he came to save a dying one. He set his ex-wife free. He set himself free from a thankless job and material greed. He did not realize until now that he set himself free to find a new love.

"There is nothing to be ashamed of. We haven't done anything to be ashamed of. Your husband was a good man," said Allan. He did not want to push her into any rash decisions *for* or *against* deepening their relationship.

"He was a good man," Mary said. Allan suspected she said this as much to reassure herself as to share it with him.

The chickens consoled them with coos. Allan wondered if chickens could actually coo, or if he only imagined their sympathy. Either way, the animals did not seem to mind sharing their space with the humans. Allan noticed a clutch of eggs still waiting to be collected. He took the empty hand-woven basket from Mary and took both of her hands in his.

He said, "I've really enjoyed our time together these past couple months. I was not looking for anybody and I did not expect more than your company." He paused. Allan knew his feelings for Mary changed spending so much time together. He did not know how much he should say though. He decided to say, "I will be here for you. If you see fit to become more than friends, I will be waiting."

Mary squeezed his hands. She said,

"Corinthians tells me that it is okay to move on from my departed husband, but only in the eyes of the Lord. It does not help me rectify my heart though. If you don't mind, I think I will forego tonight's supper. I need some time alone to pray."

Mary Reece left Allan alone to gather the eggs. Most of the other morning chores at Allan's had already been done. Allan had a few desks that needed their legs tightened over at the school, but he decided to put that off until tomorrow. He wanted to give Mary the time she needed. It would also give him some time. He figured he could use some prayer and contemplation, as well.

Encounter

As Allen walked silently out of the barn, he could still smell sawdust even though the barn was months old. It made him think about renewal. How old was the original barn, he wondered. That made him think about Tina and their many years together. They had been divorced less than a year.

Allan asked himself if it was acceptable to be moving on so fast. Maybe, he reasoned, it was not *that* fast. What he considered his last chance at a salvaged life turned out to be his first chance at a new life.

Crossing from the barn to the house, Allan

looked at the back pasture for his cows. He knew it would be time to get them back in the barn soon. Instead of cows, he saw a man standing in his field.

"Who's that?" Allan said to himself.

He hurriedly set the basket of eggs on the front porch and headed for the field. He wanted to see why a man stood in his field more out of curiosity than concern.

At this time of morning, the Karsten men would be in their own fields. Allan could not guess who it might be. From a distance, he could tell it was an outsider. The man wore cargo shorts, a baseball cap and black sunglasses, like a skier might wear. When Allan got close enough, he could see a company logo on the man's polo shirt. It read *Foresight*.

The man busied himself driving a tall pole into the ground and apparently did not notice Allan's approach.

"Greetings, friend," said Allan.

The man nodded and then whispered into a handheld radio. It sounded like he said, "Great, I got one."

Allan looked at the rest of the man's equipment lying on the ground. He understood immediately that this man was part of a survey crew. He scanned the horizon and spotted the man's partner quite a ways away. He could see the distant man hunched over, staring through the lens of his level, or possibly his theodolite.

"I'm sorry," started Allan, "but you know you're in my pasture." Ben Abrim once showed

Allan how far his property went and they were nowhere near the boundary. This could not be a simple mistake.

The surveyor said, "Look buddy, let me do my job. You go talk to your chief witch doctor or whoever's in charge."

Did Allan's plain appearance frighten the man that much? Did the man know so little about the Amish to be that prejudiced? Remembering his pledge of non-violence, Allen decided instead of arguing with the man, it would be better to talk to Elder Tibold. As he walked away, Allan caught a glimpse of a map that showed all of Karsten Field down to the highway.

Before going to the Fencil house, Allan made a detour. Allan still did not feel completely comfortable around Elder Tibold. He believed the old man had yet to truly and totally accept him. Allan did not know what else he could do to prove himself. As long as he proved his faith to God, Allan did not think it mattered what Tibold secretly believed.

The detour led Allan to Ben Abrim's front door.

"Welcome, Mr. Howarth. You're right in time for lunch," said the ever-smiling Ben Abrim.

"Do you think we could take it to go?" asked Allan.

Ben Abrim looked confused, but he agreed. He quickly slapped together two sandwiches and met Allan on the front porch.

"What troubles you?" asked Ben Abrim.

"We need to see Elder Tibold. I discovered

some outsiders trespassing on my land," said Allan.

"That is unusual for this time of year," said Ben Abrim between bites. "In the fall, we do get the occasional hunter that has lost his way."

Allan finished his sandwich in two big bites before they reached Tibold's front steps. He swallowed and then said, "My concern is that they acted like they were supposed to be there doing that survey."

"We are all right where we are supposed to be," said Ben Abrim. "Perhaps we could impose on Elder Tibold for some answers and some lemonade." Ben Abrim finished the conversation with a knock on the Fencil door.

Conclave

Mrs. Fencil ushered the two men into the front sitting room. Elder Tibold waited for them to be seated until he came into the room. Allan assumed Tibold wanted to remind them of their place.

From the light slipping past the thin white curtains, Allan thought Elder Tibold looked a little older, a little weaker. He had always been such an imposing figure to Allan. Now, for some reason, he looked defeated. Allan guessed this might have something to do with the survey crew.

"Will you tell us what's going on?" asked

Allan. He felt some confidence with Ben Abrim at his side and chose to be direct. He thought it would show more respect than playing verbal games.

Tibold Fencil lowered himself into a wide chair. He grimaced with the movement. Allan thought he heard a few joints pop.

The old man said, "First, I will tell you what I thought of you when you arrived in Karsten Field. I did not want you here. I believed you too corrupted by the outside world. You lived a life of temptation and sloth. I never expected you to have the strength to walk a righteous path."

Elder Tibold paused. His words did not surprise Allan. Elder Tibold had never been this blatant before. Still Allan knew how the old man felt by him being the last to shun Allan.

Tibold continued, "You surprised me. I do not know God's ultimate plan for you, but now I see you are meant to walk in Karsten Field for as long as it exists."

Ben Abrim looked like he wanted to jump up from his seat. He said, "What do you mean *for as long as it exists*?"

"Control yourself, Mr. Zook," demanded Elder Tibold. His fierceness returned momentarily. "Mr. Howarth is correct. There are men conducting a survey of Karsten Field. That is the beginning and end of it."

Tibold closed his eyes and spoke softly. Allan heard him say, "O our God, will you not execute judgment on them? For we are powerless against this great horde that is coming against us. We do

144

not know what to do, but our eyes are on you."

"This wasn't even a full survey crew and it sounds like you are giving up," said Allan.

The old man slowly opened his eyes and connected with Allan. Allan expected stern reprimand or possibly yelling. That is what would have happened from his boss in his old life. Then the lines on Elder Tibold's face crinkled up into a smile.

He said, "Take my yoke upon you, and learn from me, for I am gentle and lowly in heart, and you will find rest for your souls. We will not challenge the outsiders. Things have come to pass. As they came out of Israel, so shall we come out of Karsten Field. We will find a new home, perhaps in Bloomfield."

Ben Abrim shifted in his seat. The meeting had become uncomfortable for Allan too. A cool breeze snuck through the house. That gave Allan a chance to gather his thoughts. He wanted to know why they were losing the land.

Before Allan could speak, Ben Abrim said, "I knew we had some concerns with the Englishers. Hezekiah Karsten settled this land with only a handshake. A man's word may be good enough for you and me, but the outside world is run by lawyers and contracts. Tibold, it is time to tell us the whole situation. No more hiding behind scripture."

Allan looked at the man seated on his left. In his estimation, Ben Abrim had never looked so tall. He clearly had been moved by the Spirit to speak so earnestly with Tibold Fencil.

Elder Tibold's eyes widened, almost as if he had been slapped. No one ever spoke to him the way Allan and his good friend were today. He said, "I cannot tell you because I do not fully understand. Do you recall, Mr. Zook, last year when those Englishers met with me at Kinzinger's Restaurant?"

Ben Abrim nodded without a word.

Tibold continued, "They had all the papers and contracts you could imagine. I decided at that time, if God had plans for us to leave Karsten Field, then we had no other choice. They insisted that whatever agreement Hezekiah Karsten had with the original owner of this land, that it had no validity. Given our proximity to the Interstate, apparently, there is need for yet another, oh what is the word? They swim inside the building."

It took Allan a moment, but he realized what Elder Tibold wanted to say. He answered, "A waterpark? They want to build an indoor waterpark here?"

Ben Abrim's expression told Allan that he had no idea what a waterpark was.

"This is crazy," said Allan. "You can't give up your homes. Me either. We're in this together. There has to be something. Do you have any papers that prove you own this land?"

"Shortly after they changed the name to Karsten Field, all of the land became the property of the church, with one exception," said Elder Tibold.

Allan knew he meant Shepherd Tunstile's land, his land. He said, "I have a deed from Mr.

Tunstile. I know mine is legitimate because I originally planned to sell the property."

"Perhaps there are some helpful documents. We have a small collection of papers from dealings with Englishers over the years, such as our business licenses," explained Elder Tibold.

Allan stood. He felt confident that he could resolve their issue. He thought he would call one of his old co-workers. They would have access to the records and the real estate proceedings that he needed.

Tibold Fencil reached out a slightly shaky hand. Allan took it and helped the old man stand. Tibold did not let go of his grip once on his feet. He squeezed Allan's hand a little tighter.

Tibold said, "I did not trust you, but now you are our only hope."

"You know you're not the only one that can quote scripture?" said Allan. "Let not your hearts be troubled. Believe in God; believe also in me."

Ben Abrim joined the handshake by putting his hands on each of the men's shoulders. He said, "What can we do to help?"

"I need a telephone, but first, let's look at those papers," said Allan.

Parley

Kinzinger's Restaurant, in their small business district, proved to be an important site.

Not only did Elder Tibold's fateful meeting take place here, but also they maintained the only telephone in Karsten Field. Orders for food, blankets, furniture all came over this same line. Mr. Kinzinger also took the reservations for visitors staying at the two-story bed and breakfast at the end of the street.

Allan made his call. Now, he waited.

It took some convincing, but he got an old co-worker to do some research for him. He spent five minutes reminding the guy that they sat next to each other for five years. Their desks actually touched. In less than a year, it seemed no one remembered him in the outside world. Allan did not mind that at all. Luckily, he did remember his co-worker's name, James Thomas, the man with two first names. The personal connection helped Allan convince Mr. Thomas what needed to be done.

It would take some time, but Mr. Thomas promised to call him back.

Elder Tibold did not accompany Allan and Ben Abrim to Kinzinger's. He said he felt weary and needed rest. After showing the box of Karsten papers to Allan, Tibold went for a nap.

Allan found the papers he wanted. Then he and Ben Abrim rode in Ben Abrim's two-wheeled buggy down to Kinzinger's.

Mr. Kinzinger seemed excited to have two late afternoon guests. Any lunch crowd he had dispersed over an hour ago. He planned to stay open for supper to accommodate any Interstate traffic that might make the detour for a traditional Amish meal.

Kinzinger served baked chicken and honey carrots with sweet pickles. Allan tore apart the leg and thigh, enjoying every savory bite. He had only had the pickles and carrots once before when Ms. Reece made them for him. He did not have the nerve to tell Mr. Kinzinger that he preferred Mary's cooking.

Thinking of Mary took his mind away from the pending phone call. He had not given a thought as to what might happen between the two of them if they were forced to move. He knew he was attracted to her and he thought she felt the same. With them spending so much time together lately, it seemed strange that they were not dining together now.

Ben Abrim sometimes seemed to have a certain intuition. Allan guessed he might have angels speaking to him because he always seemed to have an answer for other folks' questions.

"My good friend," started Ben Abrim, "Can I look forward to seeing Ms. Reece accompany you to church next Sunday?"

Allan almost choked on a chicken bone. He replied, "It's not like that. I mean, I don't think we are to that point yet."

"You seem to be well matched," said Ben Abrim.

Allan wanted to ask how Ben Abrim knew they were starting a relationship. Obviously, they could be seen together working at the schoolhouse. Allan had a job to do. He did not think anyone knew of their evening meals or trips to his house. Especially with Alice gone to

Chicago, he had no one around to take an interest.

"I think we are quite well matched. I do enjoy her company and we get along well. Still, it is a little soon since my divorce," said Allan.

"Nothing is ever too soon or too late according to God's plan. Because it does not adhere to your timing, does not make it wrong. Yours was a divorce of the state, but not a marriage of God. For what fellowship hath righteousness with unrighteousness? Mrs. Howarth is a good woman and she will find a good man. You are becoming a righteous man and you need a righteous woman by your side," said Ben Abrim.

"But Tina and I had twenty-two years together," stammered Allan. He reached for excuses to dodge his own fear of rejection. He wanted to be with Mary, but he did not know for certain what she wanted.

"Twenty-two years?" said Ben Abrim. "That is only a fraction of a moment in God's everlasting love. Your best years are still ahead of you. As old Tibold said, you are our last hope. If we lose this land, Ms. Reece has relatives in Ohio, which will surely carry her away from you. Now take your phone call and deliver us."

Then, back in the kitchen, the phone rang.

Mr. Kinzinger emerged from the kitchen and gestured to Allan. James Thomas called with some interesting news that elated Allan. He did not attempt to explain the details to Ben Abrim at the restaurant. Instead, they rushed back to the Fencil house.

Congregation

Allan explained to both men that the church had no legal claim to Karsten Field. The *handshake deal*, while an entertaining story, had no living witnesses or documented proof. The only recourse they had was the quitclaim deed that Allan executed when he accepted his property.

"So, my original intention to sell the land may be what saves it," said Allan. "The investors need all of the ground. Without my parcel, they don't have a parking lot."

"Praise God," said Ben Abrim.

"The Lord glorifies those that glorify Him," added Elder Tibold.

Standing on Tibold Fencil's porch, the three men hugged and rejoiced. Allan had more to add. He said, "My friend also found one other piece of information that should change the contractor's mind for good. It turns out that they misfiled one of their permits."

"What does that mean to us?" asked Elder Tibold.

"Their concerns are not ours. However, the poor filing job will allow other interested parties time to state their objections. There are a couple other indoor water parks in Iowa that will frown on new competition. They can legally delay and stall any potential construction. The contractor would lose so much money in legal fees that it will be less costly to give up on his plans," said Allan.

"Does that not mean that some other entity may come along to attempt the same thing?" asked Tibold.

"You're right," said Allan. "That was the last piece of good news. My friend, James Thomas, has agreed to help. The same delay that will stop the contractors will also allow him time to settle the property rights issue. The great thing is that he is going to do it pro bono and won't cost the church anything."

Allan walked Ben Abrim home and they finished their conversation from Kinzinger's restaurant. The sun dipped below the tree line, which meant Allan would be heading home in the dark. It did not matter to him. After today's events, he felt light shining from within himself.

"Do you see how our Father works through all of us?" posed Ben Abrim. "Even when you thought you did not belong here, when you did not want to be here, God used you to ensure that we would all remain."

"I don't believe it. I never could have planned something like that. And to find the problem with the permit on top of it all," remarked Allan.

Ben Abrim climbed his steps. The wood creaked from the weight of his small frame. He turned back to Allan. His white teeth beamed through his smile even in the fading light. He said, "Believe it. These are his plans. Give your cares to the Lord and know that when you face your greatest trials that he will guide you through."

The jovial man took a step back down toward Allan to make one of the rare instances where they stood face to face.

"We were interrupted earlier when I asked you about Ms. Reece," he said.

"Now that we're not moving anywhere, I think I will let that settle for a while. She needs her time," Allan said.

"You will do no such thing," said Ben Abrim. He firmly grasped both of Allan's shoulders. In the growing dark, Ben Abrim's voice came to his as a whisper over the chirping crickets. "Trust an old man that tells you missed opportunities can be great regrets. She is not moving anywhere. You are not going to Bloomfield. Go to her. If a candle burns in her window, go to her this very night."

Confluence

Allan left his friend, feeling somewhat confused. He had to choose whether to walk home or head toward the schoolhouse. A full moon lifted itself up over the horizon. This made it easy to see the place where the dirt road turned left down the hill. Allan could simply continue going straight and be home in thirty minutes. Going down the hill would lead him to the school and Mary Reece.

As Allan stood trying to decide, he noticed the

crickets fade to silence. He could hear no frogs or owls. The slight breeze did not even make a sound winding its way through the skinny trees that marked his familiar path home. Allan had experienced this once before. Like before, he now existed in a world all to himself. He did not realize how much he missed that feeling of exaltedness until he felt it once again.

Nothing moved around him. Allan only missed two things: the voice and the deer. As if on cue, a majestic white tail deer emerged from a cluster of cedar trees. The deer did not bolt when it saw Allan. Instead, it came directly toward him and lowered its head. The last time Allan had been this close to a deer, he was afraid to touch it. This time, he felt close to it, a kindred spirit living on God's beautiful planet. Allan slowly reached out his hand, sliding gently between its regal antlers. He let his fingers glide across the creature's forehead and down toward its nose. Then the deer turned and casually headed back into the forest.

Allan waited for that warm, comforting voice. He needed guidance and wanted the voice that had led him on this journey to show him the next step.

No sound came. Nothing from inside his heart or outside his head. Only the sound of his own breathing broke through the quiet.

Without an answer or even a hint, Allan took one step toward his home. Then the voice hit him, almost physically rocking him. He had never before heard the voice so clearly.

It said, "You decide."

When Allan wanted a clear and definite answer,

he felt like it had all been put on him. He needed guidance. Before he let himself despair, he realized something. Since the day he set foot in Karsten Field, he had been receiving guidance. He gave himself to God and in return, God gave him free will. With everything he experienced, he had to make the next decision on his own. He realized the beauty of the situation to be that no matter what he decided, God would be with him.

Allan turned and marched down the hill. He strolled under the moonlight as if he was heading to the river for fishing with the Menlachs. His heart skipped a beat when he saw the orange glow of a candle illuminating Mary Reece's living room. For whatever reason, she stayed up late tonight.

Like his beating heart, Allan bounded the last ten feet in two great skips. He stood at the solid door for a moment, gathering his composure. Then he knocked. He hoped it was calm enough not to sound like a late night emergency.

"Who is it?" came Mary's voice, muffled by the wood between them.

"It's me, Allan. Can I come in?"

No response.

That made Allan more nervous than if she would have said *no*. A moment later, she turned the latch and opened the door. From the dim candle light, he could tell she had been crying again.

Mary said, "Yes, please come in. I would like that."

As Allan stepped inside, Mary slowly closed the door behind him.

CHAPTER NINE

HUMBLED

A Question

Mary Reece spent the day in prayer and contemplation. She did not know about the strangers that almost stole Karsten Field from them. She did not know how Allan saved the land by not wanting to be there in the first place.

She took her time to remember her husband's face. He had only been gone a few years, but she could not remember the color of his eyes. This caused her guilt because she could only envision Allan's strong, blue eyes. Allan always seemed to be looking into the distance. She assumed he had an eye toward the future. He appeared to be more in tune with God's plan than any man she knew. He seemed to live a blessed life and she felt like she was supposed to be a part of that.

It hurt Mary to leave him in the barn, on his knees no less. Still, she needed the time to align the feelings of her heart and the thoughts in her head. She tried to be prudent. She avoided rash decisions and followed the commandments.

She could allow herself to love again. She knew her husband would have wanted that. She knew God would not have taken him, if He did not have something else in store for her.

While Allan went from the Fencil's house to Kinzinger's restaurant and back again, Mary sat in her rocker. She alternated from bouts of crying to thankful prayers. She asked for reconciliation with the memory of her husband and rejoiced in the strength that she gained from Allan. By the time she lit her soy candle, Mary came to a place of peace in her heart. She knew she could not live in limbo between these two men.

Then a knock came at the door. It startled her because she did not expect anyone at this late hour. Despite the burning candle, the light barely illuminated the door. Mary crossed the small room cautiously.

She called to the white door that Allan had painted only the month before, "Who is it?"

"It's me, Allan. Can I come in?" She could hear him plainly, although solid oak separated them.

Mary did her best to wipe the remains of tears from her cheeks. She did not want him to think she spent the whole day crying, even though that was mostly the truth. She thought maybe she waited too long to open the door, but when she did, Allan stood patiently. He looked energized, as if the Spirit had gotten ahold of him.

"Yes, please come in. I would like that," she

finally said and moved aside to allow him entrance.

As Allan stepped inside, Mary slowly closed the door behind him. She felt anxious about what might have brought him here so late. She suspected she knew, but did not know if she wanted to admit it. Then Allan began to speak.

He said, "I'm sorry for intruding." He paused to look around the room. The solitary rocker stilled bobbed from being recently occupied. "I'm not sure what I'm doing here."

"Say what's in your heart. The Lord has given you a purpose," said Mary.

"In that case, I only have one thing to say. Only one question," said Allan.

He took off his straw hat and dropped to one knee. When he reached for Mary's hand, she gave it willingly. It did not take Allan long to ask his question, but the silence felt infinite. Mary's heart raced. She had not expected these feelings again in her life. She thanked God for Allan Howarth.

"Will you marry me?" asked Allan. He waited on the floor for her response.

Mary recounted in her head the day's contemplations, which really were months of contemplations. Had he asked her to marry him the day he saved her from the snake, she would have said *yes* with little hesitation. Now she wanted to say *yes* with no hesitation. She managed to keep her composure, however.

"Mr. Howarth, a summer wedding is unheard of," she replied.

Allan did not move from his kneeling

position. He said, "Is that a *yes*?"

Tears began streaming down Mary's face and she could do nothing to stop them. At least, this time they were tears of joy. She said, "Yes, Allan. I can say nothing but yes."

It seemed like Allan practically leaped to his feet. He grabbed Mary in his strong, but comforting embrace and lifted her from the floor. He smiled like a schoolboy. He stammered some incomprehensible words that ended with "I love you."

The words sounded strange to her hear, but only slightly stranger coming from her mouth. Beyond her control, she said, "I love you too."

Mary wondered for an instant if she meant to say it. The flushness of her cheeks and the pounding of her heart told her she did. She kissed Allan on the lips and repeated, "I love you too."

Allan kissed her back. She could feel something more in that kiss. She could feel confidence and security. She could feel passion and goodness.

Before their intimacy could lead to something more, Mary said, "I am pleased to accept your proposal, but it is no excuse for a lack of decorum. I hope it is not too late for you to return home safely."

Allan looked confused for a moment. Then understanding crossed his face. She could not admit that she wanted him to stay. At the same time, she would not want their new love to be tarnished. After the wedding, there would be plenty of time to partake of the benefits of marriage.

With one last kiss behind closed doors, Allan left Mary's house. She blew out her candle and watched from her window. The moon lit a path for Allan and she watched him until he reached the top of the hill. He seemed almost to be floating along. She guessed he shared her elation. Harvest would not come soon enough for her, but there would be plenty of time to prepare for a fall wedding.

Waiting

The summer could not pass fast enough for Allan. Knowing each sunrise brought him one day closer to Mary caused him to complete his chores with vigor. Allan thought he even noticed a jaunt in the cow's step. He wondered if his animals shared his elation.

Allan and Mary kept to their routine. They helped each other with the work at both homes. Only Ben Abrim knew of their commitment. Still, Allan could not help feeling eyes on him at church followed by whispers and smiles. He did get an extra hug or handshake, but no one said anything directly.

Mary insisted on keeping with tradition and not telling anyone of their plans. She wanted to keep her business her own. Allan suspected she also was not sure of the reaction other Karsteners might give her. Of course, Allan felt he had to tell Ben Abrim. He made sure it was alright with Mary first.

"You can tell him, but no matter what he says, do not plant any celery," said Mary.

Allan did not know what that meant. Once he talked to Ben Abrim, it became a little clearer. His old friend insisted that celery should be included with the meal, a tradition from back east that some of the elders might appreciate. Mary would have the final say on that, however.

One other person had to be told. Allan could not resist sharing the news with his daughter. Alice stayed with him, albeit for her own reasons, and she was a part of his new life. She was away in Chicago with Samuel Menlach on his rumspringa, so he would have to write her. She had written once to say they found a clean YMCA for their accommodations. Allan searched for that address and ended up writing a three-page letter. Alice's reply came saying that Samuel agreed to cut short his rumspringa so that they would be there for the wedding.

After summer break ended, the children easily fell back into their study routine. Mary shared more of the teaching responsibilities with Allan and he found himself in front of the students more often. He enjoyed their interpretations of the scripture and loved the honest simplicity of their thoughts.

The school schedule must have caused Mary to rethink their plans a little bit. One evening, she asked, "Do you think we should push back the wedding?"

"Are you having second thoughts?" Allan almost panicked. His whole body tensed.

"Not at all, mein herz," said Mary. "I am thinking instead of November, that we should wait until the children are on winter break. We might have colder weather, but it would allow us the use of the classroom and we would have fewer responsibilities at that time."

"Um, yeah, of course," said Allan. The breath came back to his chest and he released his grip on the table that he did not realize he had. The idea made sense, which made him feel a little foolish for thinking otherwise.

In September, Mary began sewing a new dress. The pattern looked to Allan to be much the same as her current church dress. The biggest difference he could see was instead of navy blue, she made the new one with light blue material.

"Why the new dress?" asked Allan. "The old one is fine." With those few words, Allan came as close as he ever had to seeing Mary Reece angry.

She explained, "First, it is customary for the bride to make her own dress. Second, the *old one*, as you say, was made for my first marriage. I do not feel that it would be appropriate to wear it." Then she looked like she might cry with her next words, "Lastly, it is becoming a bit tight in the waist."

Allan had to control himself. He knew laughter would not be the best course of action. Plain or not, he suspected talking about a woman's figure could be dangerous. From what he could tell, she had no reason to be bothered by her size. Her clothes hid the true shape of her body, but he guessed her to weigh around one hundred and twenty pounds. It occurred to him that was not what mattered. He did not love her for her body. He fell in love with her spirit and her strength. God did not give him flesh to covet, but a soul to cherish.

His words did not come out as eloquently as his thoughts. He said, "You are the perfect size for me. Besides, I think the light blue suits you."

With that, Allan did not wait for any other response. He excused himself to some imagined work in the schoolroom to avoid any accidental insults. From past experience with Tina, he expected conversations like these to end poorly for him.

The dressmaking progressed into October. Allan found it more and more difficult to keep from shouting his love to all of Karsten Field. He did visit Kinzinger's once to call Brett. He spoke quietly on the public telephone, but did not think there were any ears bent his way.

His son accepted the news like any teenage boy might. He said, "That's cool."

"Well, I'm glad you approve," said Allan with a laugh.

Brett's next question stung Allan with surprise. "Do you want me to tell Mom?" he asked.

Allan suddenly felt like he swallowed a rock, only to be stuck half way down his throat. He said, "I hadn't really thought about it."

"She asks about you every once in a while," said Brett.

"How is she doing?" asked Allan. He could

not think of anything else to say. The phone seemed a little heavier in his hand with the change of subject. He held it away from his ear as his mind wandered. The thought of Tina gave him feelings he could not quite decipher. He knew their relationship had ended years ago. Still, he felt love for her, for the mother of his children. He did not want to hurt her.

Brett said, "She's fine. Taking care of grandma, working, you know. I think she started dating some guy from work."

Those words helped Allan shake loose from his daze. It made him feel better that Tina had a life of her own. He knew they were not walking the same path, but he still felt some responsibility. The idea of her moving on from him gave Allan a sense of freedom.

"You're going to come to the wedding then?" asked Allan.

"Sure, Dad," said Brett. Allan got as much enthusiasm out of his teenager as he could have hoped. He knew his son loved him, but he also understood a boy at that age had other things on his mind than his father's personal life.

Revelation

Up until November, nobody seemed to have an idea of the marriage plans. At least, no one spoke about it. Surely, the people of Karsten Field noticed the extra time Allan and Mary spent together. He had even escorted her to church two of the last three times.

When Alice and Samuel returned early, the Menlachs wanted an explanation. Amos seemed to accept his son's explanation that the outside world had nothing to offer but temptation. Sarah Menlach could not leave it at that. She invited Allan and Alice to a homecoming meal for her son and then cornered the young couple.

"Samuel John Menlach, I expect you will tell your mother what has brought you home. I thank Gott you have come back, but I know it is not of your own plan," said Mrs. Menlach.

Both Samuel and Alice turned their eyes to Allan. He stopped chewing in the middle of a bite of baked pork. Everyone at the table now looked to Allan for an answer to Mrs. Menlach's question.

Allan washed down the mouthful with a swig of milk. He pause for a second, not wanting to share the news without Mary. "Well, we were going to announce it at church this Sunday, but Ms. Reece and I are getting married."

After the announcement, Amos and his twin sons went immediately back to eating. Katie and Annie clapped and commenced giggling. Only Mrs. Menlach seemed shocked by the news. She turned to her husband and said, "I told you. Did I not tell you? I see it in her eyes every time I see her. She is a changed woman. Gut Gott, thank you. She is a strong woman and needs a strong man."

The rest of the meal, Mrs. Menlach monopolized the conversation with wedding plans. She offered to help with the dress, the food. She offered their house for the event, without even consulting her husband.

"We are planning to use the classroom," said Allan.

Then Sarah Menlach asked a question for which Allan did not have an answer.

"In whose house will you live?" she asked.

That should have been one of the first things they discussed, Allan realized. For the second time that night, he found himself making a decision without Mary about their shared future. The answer came to him like a sudden inspiration. In retrospect, it seemed like the only obvious solution. Allan felt that he should stand for what he had to say. A few crumbs of pie fell from his shirt as he rose. He reached for his mostly empty glass of milk, as if he was making a toast.

"My thought would be that I would move into Ms. Reece's home. Seeing as we are both teachers and share the workspace, it makes sense that we would share the living space. That does leave one problem. What to do with the land and house left to me by my former teacher, Shepherd Tunstile? Again, that answer is simple."

Allan looked at his daughter. He fought back an urge to cry.

With a deep breath, Allan continued, "We have another couple among us this evening that has previously made their intentions known. As a wedding gift to Samuel and my daughter, I present them with my farm, so long as Sam helps me work it this coming spring and summer." Allan raised his glass and said, "Cheers."

Alice jumped up and hugged him. Samuel stood behind her and offered his hand. Allan pulled him close and hugged him too.

That Sunday, Allan left early for church so he could speak with Elder Tibold. The onset of cooler weather seemed to affect Tibold's health. He never fully recovered from the anxiety of nearly losing all of their homes. Allan did not like to see him like this. All the same, he asked him to announce his wedding plans.

"It is my privilege," said the old man. He patted Allan's hand and Allan could feel the roughness of years of hard, honest work. He could also feel the lack of strength. He remembered the first time he met Tibold and how tall the man seemed. Now, with a hunch to his back, they seemed about the same height.

As if he read Allan's mind, Elder Tibold said, "It is not I who have changed. You have grown in stature in the eyes of the Lord. You will stand tall in Karsten Field for some time, I think."

Union

The night before the wedding, a snowstorm covered Karsten Field in a white blanket. Allan waited at Kinzinger's for Brett's bus to arrive. Instead, he got a phone call from his son saying the storm would keep him from coming. Allan did not expect Brett to express any other interest, but Brett asked him to call after the ceremony and tell him all about it.

The snow made things a little more challenging, but preparations were well under way by five in the morning. After morning chores, Allan and Alice left their farm to help Mary in her kitchen. Mrs. Menlach and Mrs. Kinzinger had beaten them there. The massive amount of food surprised Allan. It looked like they could feed well over a hundred people. Before Ben Abrim came to counsel the couple, Mrs. Lenaxel and Mrs. Gundy arrived with more food.

Around seven o'clock, Ben Abrim took Allan and Mary from the kitchen, leaving the others to finish cooking. Elder Tibold had given his consent for Ben Abrim to minister the ceremony.

"I have very few words for the both of you. I am sure I knew this marriage would come about before either of you did. With our young people, there is more counseling to be done. Both of you walk in the light of God and have the wisdom to see what is set before you. To be sure, however, I will ask, is this union acceptable to you both?"

"It is," said Mary.

"Yes," followed Allan. He felt good that she answered so swiftly. He did not think she would back out at this point and her response pushed that thought from his mind.

After that, Allan and Mary retreated to

separate rooms to dress into their wedding clothes. Allan borrowed a suit from Matthew Fencil, plain black. He had help from Ben Abrim tying his bow tie. Allan hoped he would not wear one again, at least until Alice's wedding.

By the time he made it into the classroom, most everyone had gathered. The school desks had been stacked in front of the chalkboard, allowing for benches and tables in the center of the crowded room. The married couples kept to the outer part of the room with the young children. Per Ben Abrim's instructions, Allan helped seat and pair up a few unmarried couples. Of course, he sat Alice and Samuel across from each other. Next, he put Samuel's brother David across from June Kinzinger and Reimy Troyer across from the Miller's second oldest daughter.

When Mary Reece entered the room, everyone fell silent. Allan's heart beat hard in his chest. His palms had not sweated like they were now since high school. Mary did not need makeup, flowers or even a veil to be the most beautiful woman he had ever seen. The soft blue dress hung down past her knees and honestly did not look much different from any of her other dresses. Somehow, the color of it gave her soft skin a glow like he had never before seen on her. It made her scattering freckles stand out darker, much like her black kapp made her brown hair seem darker. Allan knew God had blessed him with a truly beautiful woman.

Ben Abrim offered a solemn sermon. He concluded by paraphrasing the Dordrecht

Confession. He said, "The Apostle Paul taught matrimony in the church, and left it free for everyone to be married, according to the original order, in the Lord, to whomsoever one may get to consent. By these words, in the Lord, there is to be understood the believers of the New Testament have no other liberty than to marry among the chosen generation and spiritual kindred of Christ, who have previously become united with the church as one heart and soul, have received one baptism, and stand in one communion, faith, doctrine and practice, before they may unite with one another by marriage. We gather today with Allan and Mary to witness, as their hearts and souls are joined with Christ, so shall they be joined together. Now, will the bride and groom please step forward?"

Mary and Allan moved up to the front of the room, holding hands. Ben Abrim clasped both of his hands around theirs. He spoke loudly and asked Allan first about his intentions. Then he asked Mary for her consent. He followed with a blessing, again from the Dordrecht. This time, he did not raise his voice as loud as he said, "We confess that there is in the church of God an honorable state of matrimony, of two free, believing persons, in accordance with the manner after which God originally ordained the same in Paradise, and instituted it Himself with Adam and Eve, and that the Lord Christ did away and set aside all the abuses of marriage which had meanwhile crept in, and referred all to the original order, and thus left it. Our Father, as you look down on these two individuals, make them one in Your sight. Join their hearts that they may glorify You for the remainder of their days."

Since there was no exchange of rings, Allan did not know what to do with the silence. He chose to kiss his new bride. Cheers and applause met his decision.

Ben Abrim added, "Go forth in the Lord's name. You are now man and wife."

More cheers led into a joyful hymn. Ben Abrim ended the ceremony with a quiet prayer. Then the smell of food wafted in from the kitchen. Fidgeting children could no longer contain themselves as the Karsten women served lunch. The feasting continued into the afternoon, interspersed with singing and an abundance of laughter.

The joy and warmth Allan felt caused him to think of another day. He imagined Alice's wedding. As a father, the thought of this day passed through his mind more than once since her birth. He knew some day, another man would take her away from him. He thanked God that she had found a worthy man. It would be almost a year yet, but Allan could already feel tears of joy welling up behind his eyes.

Set Free

Due to the coming of more snow, the

celebration ended early. Most of their friends left for home by four o'clock. Allan could not believe how little food they had left. He could not believe how much he had eaten. He could feel his stomach stretched behind his shirt buttons.

Mary wanted to start cleaning and the Menlachs stayed to help.

"You all should head home before this weather gets worse," said Allan. "Besides, I want to go to Kinzinger's to use the phone. I promised Brett I would call."

Ben Abrim stood by the door. He looked as cheerful as ever. "Do you mind if I accompany the newlyweds?"

"That is up to Ms. Re..." started Allan. He corrected himself with a grin, "Mrs. Howarth."

Mary set a stack of dirty dishes on the end of the nearest table. She wiped her hands on her apron before untying it. She said, "Mr. Zook, I would be delighted for the company. Besides, I think a walk would serve our digestion well."

Snowflakes sparkled in the dusk as the sun forced its way through torn clouds. The two sets of Menlach twins could not resist throwing snowballs as they walked up the hill toward their home. Allan, Mary and Ben Abrim waited outside for Alice and Samuel.

"Let them come when they may," said Ben Abrim. "They are good children and will not get up to any mischief."

Allan agreed and they headed toward Kinzinger's restaurant. The snow did not prove as fierce as the previous night making the walk almost pleasant. At the moment, Allan walked with his two best friends and he would soon be sharing the day's events with his son. The Lord had delivered a very good day and Allan could not have been happier.

They turned the corner onto the main street. Allan dug in his pocket for the key that Mr. Kinzinger had been kind enough to lend him. Ben Abrim stopped for a moment and that caught Allan's attention.

His old friend said, "You realize, Mr. Howarth, that it was one year ago today that we met almost in this very spot?"

Allan did not realize that. If Ben Abrim had not chosen to walk with them, the moment would likely have gone unnoticed. As it was, Allan took the opportunity to hug the ever-smiling man.

"Thank you for being a great friend," said Allan.

"I hope I have been a great teacher, as well. I give thanks to the Lord that you are so much more than Mr. Tunstile ever promised you'd be. Please know that I will be there to show you the right path whenever I can," said Ben Abrim.

A cold shiver from Mary caused the men to resume their walk. Allan read the sign on Kinzinger's front door as he unlocked it. *Closed for Wedding*. This made Allan smile. He thought nothing could make him stop smiling this day.

The tarnished bell above the door chimed as the three friends walked into the dining room. A moment later, the bell rang once more. Allan turned, expecting to see Alice and Samuel's flush red cheeks. Instead, a stranger greeted them.

"Hey guys. I ran out of gas and was looking for help. I thought I saw some lights from the highway, so I walked up here. When I saw you folks, I yelled," said the stranger.

"We heard no yelling," said Ben Abrim.

The stranger moved into the room, looking toward the kitchen. He said, "Yeah, well, maybe I wasn't loud enough. Is anyone back there?"

Allan stepped between the stranger and Mary. Something made him uneasy about this man that appeared from nowhere. He did not think it likely that any lights could be seen from the interstate since all of the shops were closed today. Besides, if he ran out of gas, Allan asked himself, why would he come so far away from the highway?

"There's no one here but us," Allan said.

The stranger used his left hand to brush his shoulder length hair out of his face. The clinging snowflakes melted, leaving a wet shine. With his right, he reached into his denim jacket and retrieved a large hunting knife.

The stranger pointed the tip of the knife over Allan's shoulder directly at Mary. He said, "That's fine. We can start with the cash register here. Then give me the keys to the other shops."

Allan wanted to rush the stranger. He believed he could knock the knife out of the stranger's gloved hand. This man had to be at least fifty pounds lighter than Allan, so he thought he could easily send him to the ground.

Before he could move, Ben Abrim put a hand

on Allan's shoulder. He said, "Step back, Allan. If your enemy is hungry, feed him; if he is thirsty, give him something to drink."

"Yeah, you boys step back," said the stranger. "Not you lady. You get me the money."

The stranger moved like a traffic director, giving instructions with a shining steel blade. He separated Allan from his new wife. Allan understood his pledge of non-violence. He and Ben Abrim discussed it at length when Brett once mentioned joining the Marines for a computer scholarship.

He whispered to Ben Abrim, "I have to do something."

"You have no assurance that your actions would improve the situation," said Ben Abrim. "We must not inflict pain, but seek salvation. Deliverance will come."

As Ben Abrim said this, the doorbell jingled a third time. The appearance of the stranger caused Allan to forget they were being followed. The sudden movement must have startled the stranger. The desperate man spun around wildly. His blade slashed Sam Menlach on the shoulder and cut clean through his wool coat. Samuel fell back against the door and slid down to the ground. Then the stranger grabbed Alice by the hair and backed up to the wall.

"Nobody move. Don't do it," demanded the stranger.

Allan could barely contain himself. First, the man threatens his wife and now he holds Alice's life in his hands. There had to be a point when violence was acceptable, forgivable, he thought. Surely, the Lord would not turn a day of joy into a day of sorrow. He believed he had the power to stop this, but his inaction made it worse. Allan wanted to charge at the stranger. Ben Abrim stopped him again.

Ben Abrim spoke to the stranger. He took a step forward and said, "Young man, I know you are troubled. My Father can give you peace and lift the weight from your heart."

"Stay where you are, old man," ordered the stranger.

Ben Abrim took another step. He now stood within an arm's reach. Allan thought he could take the stranger now that he was distracted. Instead, he watched in awe as Ben Abrim moved closer to the man.

The stranger looked on the verge of panic. He held Alice with a fully extended arm, like a schoolboy pulling her pigtails except so much worse. He said, "If you don't give me the money, I'm going to cut her."

With a final step, Ben Abrim intercepted the stranger's weapon. Panic seemed to swallow the room. Allan watched the knife as the stranger plunged it into Ben Abrim's stomach. He thought he heard Ben Abrim say, "Then put the sword into the sheath."

The stranger released the knife handle and Ben Abrim fell backward, knocking over a chair. Allan rushed to his friend and pulled the knife from his side.

"That wasn't supposed to happen," uttered

the stranger. "I didn't mean it. Why did he do that?"

Mary grabbed a hand full of towels from the kitchen and rushed to help Allan. Neither of them knew how to stop the bleeding. More than ever, Allan wanted to grab the stranger and pummel him. Then he felt a hand on his collar. Allan looked down into the fading eyes of his friend.

"Do not let my sacrifice be in vain. I do not fear death, but I fear you losing your way after you have come so far."

Behind Allan, the stranger dropped to his knees. He kept muttering amid tears. He appeared to be genuinely sorry for his actions. "Dear Lord, please forgive me. I need money to feed my children. I never meant for this to happen. I so am sorry, God."

As Allan held Ben Abrim's head on his lap, he stared at the stranger. He vaguely noticed Alice race out the door for help. Samuel managed to pull himself up into a chair and press a cloth napkin over his injured shoulder. The stranger did not move. He did not try to get the money and he did not attempt to flee. Tears streamed down the man's face as he continued to pray for forgiveness.

Outside, snow fell silently.

CHAPTER TEN

FIVE YEARS LATER

One

Allan often thought back to his wedding night. Such a wonderful day came to such a tragic end. Ben Abrim almost died that night. He almost lost a dear friend. State Troopers came for the stranger.

About a year later, they received a letter from the man. In it, he again asked for forgiveness. He explained that he was about to receive parole and would be allowed to see his wife and children after a stay at a halfway house. He thanked Ben Abrim for showing him a different way. He wrote that he had given his life to Christ and his family not only supported him, but also joined him.

Ben Abrim's wound healed, but left him with a limp. He and Allan had many conversations about that night. They talked of all the possibilities. Allan realized that the little man saved him. If he had attacked that stranger, he

179

would have destroyed everything he had become. Worse than tarnishing his marriage, he would have broken his promise to God.

The following November, they celebrated Alice and Samuel's wedding. Allan invited Tina and she came. Of course, Brett could not miss his sister's wedding. Tina managed to congratulate Allan on his new marriage. He suspected it might have been awkward for her, but she did not seem bothered.

Turning over the house proved more difficult than Allan expected. It stayed mostly empty the past year. About once a week, they came for general upkeep. Ben Abrim kept Allan's cows at his place, much closer to the school. Alice lived with Allan and Mary until her wedding. When Allan passed the farm to Samuel Menlach, as promised, he made certain to file the papers to make it official.

Allan stood with his pregnant wife one last time on the porch of the house that first brought him to Karsten Field. A month later, they would have a son and name him after Ben Abrim Zook.

Two

Tibold Fencil left Karsten Field in the summer. One of his last requests was for Ben Abrim to become the elder.

Among the men at his bedside, Allan heard

the old man's final words. Much was not in English, but Allan did understand when Tibold said, "Thank you God for sending us Allan Howarth."

Allan had not witnessed an Amish funeral before now. He helped dig the grave alongside his old teacher, Shepherd Tunstile, and other past members of Karsten Field. The rows of identical tombstones made Allan realize that they were all the same in life, death and in the eyes of God.

Mr. Esch, from the furniture store, built a simple coffin. They held the ceremony in the front room of the Fencil house. Allan remembered sitting here the day they almost lost all of their homes.

Ben Abrim gave both sermons during the two-hour ceremony. He quoted the Dordrecht, "We believe with the heart that in the last day all men who shall have died, and fallen asleep, shall be awaked and quickened, and shall rise again, through the incomprehensible power of God; and that they, together with those who then will still be alive, shall be changed in the twinkling of an eye, at the sound of the last trumpet. They shall be placed before the seat of judgment, and the good be separated from the wicked; that then everyone shall receive in his own body according to that he hath done, whether it be good or evil; and that the good or pious shall be taken up enter into life eternal, and obtain that joy, which eye hath not seen, nor ear heard, neither hath entered into the heart of man, to reign and triumph with Christ forever and ever."

Matthew Fencil drove the wagon that carried his father's worldly vessel to their cemetery. Allan had never been to this part of Karsten Field. Obscured by a row of trees, the cemetery sat on top of a wide-open hill. Sun warmed the grass and the tops of the tombstones. Allan spotted one with the name of Isaac Karsten and he knew it lay empty.

He also knew that someday, there would be one with his name on it. He planned to enjoy life and glorify God until the Lord called him home.

Three

Samuel and Alice announced a pleasant surprise. Alice was pregnant and it turned out to be twins. She would not give birth until the following January, but she named the boy Isaac and the girl after her mother's middle name, Elizabeth.

That same year, Tina remarried. She met a man at her Saturday Bible study. After almost three years of dating, they were married at their church.

Four

Brett graduated high school. He did not join the marines. He honored his father's wishes to practice non-violence. Brett got a scholarship to a video game design college in Michigan.

The distance meant Brett could not visit as often. Still, Allan gave praise that Brett found a positive direction in life and could pursue something for which he had a gift.

In the summer, the stranger returned to Karsten Field. This time, he came with penance in his heart and children at his side. That cold December night changed this man's life for the better. In front of all of the Karsteners, he dropped to his knees and asked forgiveness of Ben Abrim.

"Of course, I forgive you," said a smiling Ben Abrim. "Had I not survived that night, I still would have forgiven you. Death is not the end and I would be safe in my God's arms. It is my greatest joy to see you have beaten your sword into a ploughshare. You have learned a new solution to your worries. Share that with everyone you meet."

Five

Life continued in Karsten Field.

Allan and Mary shared teaching duties. Their five-year-old son Benjamin made going to class that much more enjoyable. In only a few years, their grandchildren would be joining them.

Allan learned much about life in those few, short years. His beard grew long, with no sign of gray. He had not yelled or growled in years. He witnessed birth. He witnessed death. He witnessed his own renewal. In his heart, he firmly believed it all to be God's gift, something everyone could receive if they opened their hearts. He counted every day a blessing and found the peace he had sought for so long.